COLLECT ALL THE
INVISIBLE DETECTIVE'S
AMAZING ADVENTURES!

WEB OF ANUBIS
THE PARANORMAL PUPPET SHOW
GHOST SOLDIERS
KILLING TIME
FACES OF EVIL

All Simon & Schuster books are available by post from:
Simon & Schuster Cash Sales. PO Box 29
Douglas, Isle of Man IM99 1BQ
Credit cards accepted.
Please telephone 01624 836000
fax 01624 670923, Internet
http://www.bookpost.co.uk or email:
bookshop@enterprise.net for details

THE INVISIBLE DETECTIVE
SHADOW BEAST

BY JUSTIN RICHARDS

SIMON AND SCHUSTER

Acknowledgements

*I am indebted to my family – Alison, Julian
and Christian – for their patience, comments
and love, and to my editor, Stephen Cole,
for his comments, patience and confidence.*

SIMON AND SCHUSTER

This edition published in Great Britain by Simon & Schuster UK Ltd, 2005
First published in Great Britain by Pocket Books,
an imprint of Simon & Schuster UK Ltd 2003
A Viacom company

1 3 5 7 9 10 8 6 4 2

Simon & Schuster UK Ltd
Africa House
64-78 Kingsway
London WC2B 6AH

A CIP catalogue record for this book is available from the British Library

ISBN 0 689 86101 X

Typeset by SX Composing DTP, Rayleigh, Essex

For Julian and Alice,
two latter-day Cannoniers

Chapter 1

The police whistle was harsh in the quiet of the evening. The shrill sound split the misty September air and startled Art Drake.

He was walking home from Cannon Street station, where he had met his father off the train back from work. His dad stiffened, immediately alert. But then, he was used to the sound, listened out for it even in his sleep probably. He was already turning, trying to work out where the blasts of the whistle were coming from.

'Lombard Street?' Art suggested.

'Could be,' Dad agreed. 'A police whistle. But not a policeman blowing it. The blasts are too long – a good way to waste your breath to no useful effect.'

They were hurrying along the street now in the direction of the sound. The whistle seemed to be getting fainter if anything.

'Are you sure it's this way?' Art asked.

'I told you, he's losing his breath. You were right, Lombard Street.' Art's dad broke into a run and Art stumbled hastily after him.

Art was tall for his fourteen years, with a round face and a high forehead. His dark hair was slicked back and he shook his head to get it out of his eyes as he ran. 'A bank robbery?' he asked as he caught up. 'But aren't the banks closed on Saturdays?'

His dad nodded. 'The managers all have police whistles. Just in case.' In case of what, he did not say. 'The bank may be closed, but someone's working today.'

They turned at last into Lombard Street and now Art could see the man with the whistle. His face was round and red. He had a dark beard flecked with grey and almost no hair. Through the mist it looked as if his face was on upside-down. His shoulders hunched forwards as he blew. Behind the man a uniformed policeman was emerging at a run from a side turning.

They arrived at the same time – Art, his father and the policeman. They were all almost as out of breath as the man with the whistle. He straightened up as they approached, glaring at Art and his father before turning to the policeman.

'Thank heavens, Constable. There's been a robbery – quick!'

The man gestured for the policeman to follow and hurried into the building behind him. It was an imposing stone structure with steps up to the main entrance. The doors were heavy wood with glass set into them and brass handles. 'Hanbury and Hedges Bank' it said on a polished plate beside the door. Next to this Art saw there was a date etched into one of the large stones – 1836. So it was exactly 100 years old.

The bearded man paused as he pulled the door open and glared back at Art and his father again. The policeman paused too and looked properly at them for the first time.

Then he stepped deferentially aside and gestured for them to go ahead of him. 'Excuse me, sir,' he said politely. 'Didn't see you there.'

'That's quite all right, Wilkins,' Art's dad told him as he made for the door.

But the man with the whistle and the red face did not move, still glared back at them. 'Where do you think you're going?' he demanded.

Art looked at his dad, expecting an outburst of indignation. But his father's voice was calm and quiet.

'My apologies, sir,' he said. 'I understood

3

you were in need of police assistance.'

The man continued to stare and PC Wilkins shifted uneasily on the step below. The policeman cleared his throat, as if embarrassed. 'This is Sergeant Drake, sir,' he told the glaring man. 'Detective Sergeant Drake of Scotland Yard.'

Art tried not to grin as the man's beard seemed to open up to display a set of surprised teeth.

Art had never been in a bank vault before. The man with the beard was Neville Hanbury and, having embarrassed himself by almost excluding a Scotland Yard detective from the bank, he now seemed unwilling to exclude his son. He watched Art through narrowed eyes but said nothing.

The bank foyer was an impressive marble-floored area with a domed ceiling. Hanbury locked the doors behind them and, still breathing heavily, scurried across to a staircase on the far side. Next to the staircase was a metal grille and, as they approached, Art could see that it was in fact a lift cage. The lift was already waiting. Art pulled the heavy grille closed behind them, since nobody else seemed about to do it. At once the lift lurched into life and started to descend.

'I always do the accounts for the week on a Saturday,' Hanbury was saying. His voice was nasal and nervous. His beard twitched when he spoke, but otherwise there was no visible clue where the sound was coming from. 'I don't usually have cause to check the vault.' He shook his head in disbelief. 'To think that it might have gone undiscovered until Monday. They must have broken in this morning, while the bank was empty.'

'I didn't see any signs of a break-in, sir,' PC Wilkins said, glancing at Art's dad.

'Well, you wouldn't,' Hanbury countered with annoyance. 'Not up there.'

'Where, then?' Art's father asked.

The lift had stopped and Art pulled at the metal doors. They creaked and clanked as they swung open.

'See for yourself,' Hanbury said miserably.

Stepping out of the lift, they realised immediately what he meant. The heavy metal door to the vault was standing open, so they could see into the whitewashed brick area, deep under the bank. There was a main concourse, with vaulted alcoves off to each side. The alcoves had

5

metal gratings over them, like prison cells, but many of these had been wrenched open. The shelves inside the intact alcoves held carefully organised metal boxes, bundles of banknotes, even bars of gold.

But the alcoves where the doors had been forced open were less neatly arranged. Notes and coins were strewn across the floor, a gold bar lay on its side in the middle of the main room. A broken necklace was on the ground close to where Art was standing, pearls from its string lying in a trail back to one of the alcoves. Other items of jewellery were scattered across the vault.

'It'll take for ever to tidy up,' Hanbury said, clasping his hands anxiously in front of him. 'Sorting out what goes in which deposit box will be a nightmare.' He shook his head sadly. 'The latest locks from de Vries and Boucher as well. For all the good they were.'

'Do you have any idea how much is missing?' Art's father asked as he made his way carefully along the length of the vault.

'That's the strange thing. There isn't that much that seems to have gone. I haven't touched anything of course, but so far as I can see it's mainly notes. Cash. There's an awful lot of more valuable stuff in plain sight that hasn't been taken.'

'Perhaps they couldn't get through the gates?' Wilkins suggested.

'They got through some of them with no problem,' Sergeant Drake pointed out. 'I assume they're all the same?'

Hanbury nodded. 'Different keys, of course. But the same type of lock.'

'And they've been forced open,' Art said. 'They didn't pick the locks.' They were passing an alcove where gold bars were stacked, the door intact. 'But they didn't even try this one.'

'Our share of the Bank of England reserve,' Hanbury said as they paused to look at the gleaming wall of gold. 'They keep a proportion of it in other banks to minimise risk…' His voice tailed off. 'Thank goodness that's safe,' he murmured.

'You think they were disturbed?' Wilkins asked.

'I heard nothing,' Hanbury said. 'Quiet as the grave when I came down here. I'd have heard them running off, I think. And forcing the doors wouldn't have been a quiet job.'

'I agree.' Peter Drake blew out a long breath and looked round at the mess. 'But it does look as if they were disturbed. Or just became frightened and left. Any idea how they got in and out?'

Art was still walking, almost at the end of the huge vault now. 'I have,' he said.

'Yes,' Hanbury agreed, 'it's, er, it's not hard to miss when you get down to the bottom here.'

The last alcove on the opposite side to the main door had been completely emptied. The metal gate was hanging almost sideways where it had buckled the lower hinge under its weight. Beyond it they could now all see the gaping black hole in the wall. Bricks and fragments of cement were scattered across the floor where the brickwork had collapsed, pushed in from the other side.

The smell hit them as soon as they stood taking in the sight.

'What is that?' Wilkins said, his face scrunched up in revulsion.

'Smells like drains,' Art said, trying not to gag on the stench.

'It is,' his father said. 'Whoever they were, they tunnelled in from the main sewers.'

'Money down the drain,' Hanbury said sadly. He did not seem to be joking.

* * *

The following Monday, just like every other Monday, Brandon Lake – the Invisible Detective – held his consulting session. As ever, it was in a room above the locksmith's shop on Cannon Street. The evenings were drawing in, though it was still warm and humid in London, and the curtains twitched and rippled in the breeze. The sounds of the street outside filtered through the open window, but there was little light except that given out by the electric lamp on the table close to the door.

Flinch was standing behind the curtain. Usually she found the sessions boring – lots of talk and hushed whispers of excitement. She enjoyed being a part of it, but after a few minutes she generally got to fidgeting. Then Meg would glare at her in that disapproving manner she had perfected. Jonny was more understanding. He seemed to know that you couldn't expect a girl of Flinch's age to stand still and silent behind a curtain for hours.

Not that Flinch knew how old she was. Nor did anyone else. She might be eleven or she might be thirteen. She liked to consider herself twelve. There was a nice roundness to the number – a dozen. She was a thin girl, her clothes grubby and torn. Her long blonde hair was tangled and stained almost brown. It blew gently in sympathy with the curtain as Flinch shuffled her feet.

But for once, Meg seemed not to notice. The older girl was listening to the Invisible Detective. It was her job to know whether people were telling the truth or not. If Flinch leaned forward and peered round the curtain, she could see the silhouette of the back of the chair in which the detective sat, obscured from everyone's view. She could see the hand that appeared now and again to punctuate a point. He was talking about the bank robbery.

There had been talk of little else in the area for the last two days. News travelled fast, especially when it was sensational and supposed to be secret. A daring bank robbery – some said it was raiders with guns, others that is was a little old man who had picked the most modern locks and let himself in. Someone suggested the police had actually caught the robbers in the act and that was why there was nothing to see from the outside. Case closed. But whatever had really happened, everyone agreed on one thing – that the Invisible Detective would know.

And so he did.

'Obviously the events are still a matter of police investigation,' the detective told them in his deep voice. 'I cannot reveal all the details ahead of any possible court case.' There were a few gasps at this, and those who believed in the crooks-already-caught version of events nodded knowingly.

By now Flinch knew as much as she wanted to, so she watched the shapes of the people standing listening as they jostled for a better view of the back of the chair or leaned forward to hear more clearly. She could see Jonny doing the same, his angular features stark against what light there was, and his short hair even blacker than usual. As he listened, he rested his hand on Meg's shoulder, so that it disappeared into her dark curls. Instinctively Meg shrugged it off and Jonny stiffened with embarrassment. Flinch smiled.

'But I can tell you,' the Invisible Detective was saying, 'that there was indeed a break-in at Hanbury and Hedges Bank on Lombard Street last Saturday morning. In fact, break-in is an apt description, since the robbers tunnelled in from the sewers.'

This information provoked gasps and whispers. As people turned to one another, Flinch saw a man step into the room. She could not see him clearly, but he was looking round apprehensively, as if unsure about whether he had come to the right place.

'I cannot say what was taken, or give you more details than that at this time, I'm afraid. But the police have several very promising leads.' The detective paused. 'Now, if there are no further questions?' People were already edging towards the door at the top of the stairs, ready to resume their whispered conversations at greater length and greater volume elsewhere.

Flinch could see the new man more clearly now as he was standing close to the table-lamp. He was short and stocky, perhaps fifty years old, with greying hair. 'I have a question,' he said. His voice was husky and hesitant, but it had the effect of stopping everyone at once. 'Er, if that's all right.' He looked round. 'I'm not really sure how this works, I'm afraid.'

A large man close beside him answered. Flinch could see that it was Albert Norris, the publican at the Dog and Goose on Cannon Street. 'You put sixpence on the plate,' he explained. 'Then you can ask your question. And the detective will answer it next week.'

There was a sense of hushed anticipation as the crowd wondered what calamity or puzzle had brought someone who did not know the procedure – someone from outside the area who was evidently concerned and nervous. A clink could be heard as the man's sixpence dropped on to the plate. He cleared his throat.

'Well,' he said, 'my name's Fredericks and I live round the back of St Swithin's Lane.' He paused, his feet shuffling nervously. Flinch was holding her breath. 'It's like this,' the man went on. 'I know it sounds silly, but I'm worried about my Tiger.'

This drew a gasp from several people. Flinch leaned out from behind the curtain, ignoring Meg's urgent wave for her to get back out of sight.

'Your tiger?' the detective asked, his voice slightly higher-pitched than usual.

'That's right. Well, he's been missing for a few days now, you see.' Mr Fredericks was looking round in apparent embarrassment.

'Tiger's just his name, of course, because of his colouring and the dark stripes. He's my pet cat.'

There was a pause, then someone laughed. Before long, most people had joined in, pushing past the bemused Mr Fredericks as they headed for the stairs. Flinch watched them go, then studied the short, stocky man standing in the middle of them. She blinked, thinking of the cat lost out on the London streets. 'Oh, the poor thing,' she murmured.

Meg was always amused by Flinch's different sense of priorities. While she and Jonny were interested in the daring bank robbery, Flinch was concerned for something as mundane as a missing cat. But maybe that was because Flinch lived on the streets – had always lived on the streets, for as long as Meg or Jonny or even Art could remember. And also because, whatever Meg's own home life might be like, at least she had a home, unlike Flinch, who lived in the disused warehouse on a corner of Cannon Street that the Cannoniers used as a den. Flinch's home was among the decaying rolls of carpet that were still piled up in the derelict building. Perhaps, after all, Flinch's feelings for a lost cat forced to live in the open and scavenge for its food were better informed than Meg's interest in a sensational robbery that had only really hurt people's wallets.

Of course, Meg and Jonny and Art brought stuff from their own homes for Flinch when they could. And any small profits from Brandon Lake's sessions went towards looking after their friend. It added to the excitement of the children's enterprise that there was a practical value to the Invisible Detective as well as the sheer fun of it all.

Jonny counted the money on the plate as Meg checked that everyone had gone. 'I need a drink of water,' said the figure seated in the armchair. But it was not the voice of Brandon Lake, the Invisible Detective – because, quite simply, he did not exist. Instead it was a voice that was younger, less serious – the voice of a fourteen-year-old boy. 'It makes your throat dry, all that talking in a deep voice,' Art went on. He heaved himself out of the chair and shrugged off the oversized coat. 'I nearly had a coughing fit as well at the end there.'

'I don't think Mr Jerrickson dusts up here very often,' Jonny said. 'Or at all, come to that. I've got his rent for the room here, and we made one and six profit this week.'

Art nodded. 'That's good,' he said. 'Where's Flinch?' They all turned to look for her, but the young girl had gone.

'She did say something,' Jonny told them, 'about going to see a man about a cat.'

Arthur Drake was looking at a half-completed crossword when the bottom fell out of his world. A week ago he would have been anxious to avoid visiting his grandfather in the home, but now he was intrigued by the old man. A lot had happened in that week.

It all started when Arthur was given a strange stone and an old notebook. The stone reminded him of a poem they had read at school – it had 'colours of the moon', and he could lose himself staring into its depths. But it was the notebook that was really of interest – *The Casebook of the Invisible Detective*, written in the 1930s. He took it everywhere, reading and re-reading the yellowing, handwritten pages whenever he got a chance.

Arthur looked again at the crossword in the paper, at the way the capital letters in the answers were formed. His grandfather's handwriting was identical to his own. And it was because it seemed to be written in his own handwriting that Arthur had first been drawn to the notebook. That and the fact it was written by someone who shared his name.

'I can't get three across,' Grandad was saying as Arthur continued to stare at the paper. The old man pulled himself to his feet and walked over to join the boy, looking down at the clues.

'I told you Arthur is an old family name.' Arthur's dad was saying. He was responding to a question of Arthur's, a question about how someone with his handwriting and his name could have lived at the same address where he himself now lived with Dad. Dad laughed. 'Arthur Drake, meet your namesake.'

Grandad's mouth twitched with amusement and the wrinkles round his eyes seemed to deepen. Arthur just stared.

'You mean...'

'We named you after Grandad, after my father here,' Dad said.

17

'Arthur Drake,' Arthur said, so quietly he could barely hear his own voice.

'That's right,' Grandad replied in a voice that was almost as quiet. 'But my friends call me Art for short.'

'So you're the Invisible Detective,' Arthur whispered, just loud enough for his grandfather to hear.

Across the room Arthur's dad was staring out of the window, oblivious. Grandad simply smiled.

Chapter 2

Someone else got to Mr Fredericks before Flinch.
She had followed him down the stairs and out
across Cannon Street. She was upset at the way
people had laughed – just because a lost cat was
not as exciting as a bank robbery. She wanted to
tell the man that she knew it was at least as
important. The bank robbery had hurt no one, Art
had said. But Tiger could be in pain and might
need help. It wasn't funny, she wanted to assure
him, and the Invisible Detective would find his
poor cat.

But before she could run across to the turning
off Cannon Street into St Swithin's Lane, a car
veered noisily across the road in front of her. It
shrieked to a halt close beside the startled Mr
Fredericks and a man leaped out of the back.

Flinch crossed behind the car, trying to edge
close to the two men as they spoke. From the look
on Mr Fredericks's face, he was frightened. The
other man was wearing a top hat and a heavy
charcoal-grey coat with the collar turned up. But
Flinch could see that his hair was greasy and

black and stuck out in tufts between hat and collar. The man's face was swarthy and he had sideburns that reached down to the level of his chin. His lips were thin and pale as he spoke quietly to Mr Fredericks.

Mr Fredericks's answer was louder, and by now Flinch was closer and could make out some of what he was saying. 'Don't worry, I'll get it back. It can't have strayed far.'

Flinch froze, pressed against the wall and hoping that neither man would notice her. They must be talking about the cat.

'You had better,' the man in the top hat hissed. His voice dropped and Flinch could make out only a few odd words as he leaned close to the obviously terrified Mr Fredericks. '…your own ends,' the man finished, his voice rising in anger. 'The project is too important for that.' Then his voice was lost behind the sound of a passing taxi. '…underground,' Flinch caught as the taxi chuntered into the distance. 'Whatever it takes.' The man turned back towards his car. The engine was still idling and the driver watched them through the side window.

'Don't worry,' Mr Fredericks called

nervously after the man. 'Tell Gibson I'll get it back, I promise.' He took a step towards the car. 'I've got the Invisible Detective…' But the rest of his words were lost as the car pulled rapidly back on to the road and sped away.

Mr Fredericks watched it disappear into the distance. Then he turned back towards St Swithin's Lane. For a moment his eyes rested on Flinch. She wondered if she should say something – *what* she should say. But he seemed not to have noticed her and continued on his way. She watched him walking slowly, head down, along the lane until he reached an archway. She ran quickly after him.

The other side of the archway was a small courtyard with two tiny houses set at right angles to each other. One was boarded up and derelict. Flinch was just in time to see Mr Fredericks going into the other one, closing the door firmly behind him.

'You didn't say anything to him?' Art asked.

Flinch shook her head. 'Didn't know what to say.'

Art, Meg and Jonny had arrived back at the

den just ahead of Flinch. Art had listened with amusement as she struggled breathlessly to get out her story. When she had finished, Flinch flopped down on a threadbare roll of carpet, sending a cloud of dust into the air. There was a streetlight outside one of the grimy windows and its pale, smudged light struggled through the dusk outside to illuminate the huge warehouse area.

Art nodded. 'Just as well perhaps. Until we know what's going on. This cat is obviously more important than just any old stray pet.'

'He wasn't lying though, was he?' Jonny asked Meg.

'That's a point,' Art said. 'After all, you'd know.'

Meg could tell immediately if someone was lying. It was a knack that had helped the Invisible Detective's investigations on more than one occasion.

Meg frowned as she considered this. 'No,' she said at last, shaking her head so that her curled red hair caught the light and seemed to glow. 'No, he wasn't lying. But he may not have been telling us the whole truth.'

'A missing cat.' Jonny sighed. 'Where do we start?' He looked at Art. 'Your dad doesn't keep a list of stray cats or anything, does he?'

'Hardly the concern of Scotland Yard's finest,' Art admitted. 'And anyway, he has a few other things on his plate at the moment.'

'Like the robbery, you mean?' Meg said.

'Yes, what's happening about that?' Jonny asked. 'You mentioned some promising leads.'

'I think our friend Brandon Lake, the Invisible Detective, was embellishing slightly there,' Art admitted, to Meg and Jonny's obvious disappointment. 'As far as I can tell, they don't have anything much to go on at all. Dad said they've boarded up the tunnel into the vault. But they don't want to fix it permanently until they're sure they aren't missing something.' He paused dramatically before adding, 'And then, of course, there's the murder.'

The expression on Jonny's face was priceless. Meg just frowned, as usual, and Flinch seemed not to be paying attention at all. But Jonny's jaw dropped and his eyes widened. 'Murder!'

Art laughed. 'Don't get too excited. But yes, Dad's got a murder to investigate now as well.'

'Who was murdered?' Meg asked.

Art shrugged. 'Some old man. Found on that

waste ground down between the gasworks and the river with a knife in his back.'

Jonny snorted in disappointment. 'Some tramp, probably. Killed by another tramp for a bottle of whisky or something.'

'Probably,' Meg agreed quietly. 'It's the drink that does it.'

They were silent for a few moments after that. Then Flinch spoke. Her voice was quiet and she was staring into the darkness at the back of the warehouse.

'That boy who got lost, the one we found fallen into the storm drain by the river,' she said. 'He told me there was a dead cat down in there with him. Maybe it was Tiger.'

'Andrew Baxter his name was. But that was a long time ago, Flinch,' Art said gently.

'Still,' Jonny told her, 'it's the only lead we've got.'

When they had found the boy all those weeks ago, Flinch had had to squeeze through a hole in the wall to get from an enclosed yard down to the storm drain by the river. But when the police had come to help the boy out, they had cut through an alleyway further north that led directly to the riverside. This was the route the Cannoniers took that Monday evening.

It was almost dark when they arrived at the bricked opening in the ground that was the drain. Art could see that Meg was getting nervous about the time. 'We'll make this as quick as we can,' he said.

Jonny had brought a torch and Art had a length of rope he had found in the warehouse.

'That will never hold your weight,' Meg told him as Art measured out the rope and peered down into the dark opening.

'It doesn't have to,' he told her.

Meg stared at him, anger creeping on to her face. 'You'd better not be thinking of lowering Flinch down there.'

'I don't mind,' Flinch said brightly. 'Though it pongs a bit.'

'More than a bit,' Jonny agreed.

Meg was still staring at Art, her hands on her hips, as if daring him to disagree with her. He couldn't help but laugh. 'Don't worry. I'm going to lower something, but it isn't Flinch.' He saw Meg's eyes widen. 'And it isn't you or Jonny either.'

'What, then?'

'The light.' Art began to tie the torch to the end of the rope. 'We'll be able to see from up here if Tiger's down there. He'll see the light and make some sound in any case. But I agree, I don't think any of us should have to climb into the sewers in the dark.'

They watched the light as it swung and bobbed its way down into the drain. It was only about ten feet deep and almost at once they could see the inky water reflecting the torchlight. Moments later they could see shapes floating in the water, breaks in the reflection.

When the light reached almost to the bottom and they could all see clearly, Flinch turned away. Jonny blew out a long breath. Meg closed her eyes.

Art found himself counting. Seven that he could see. 'Seven dead cats,' he said out loud.

'I don't think Tiger's down there,' Flinch said quietly from somewhere behind him. 'I didn't see a stripy cat.'

She was right. Art forced himself to look at each of the bedraggled bodies that half floated in the dark water at the bottom of the drain. None of them, so far as he could tell, had prominent dark stripes. But each and every one of them had been ripped to pieces.

The mobile phone sounded extraordinarily loud in the small room. Both Arthur and his grandfather looked up, startled.

Arthur's dad smiled apologetically as he checked the number of the caller and answered. 'Drake here,' he said in a tone that Arthur knew he reserved for work calls. His dad gave Arthur and Grandad a wave and, with the phone pressed to his ear, let himself out of the room.

'Police business,' Arthur said. 'He doesn't like being overheard.'

'Some people,' Grandad said with a smile, 'seem to have a mobile phone for the sole purpose of being overheard when they are using it.' He put down the paper on the bedside cabinet. 'I don't think we're going to get that last clue,' he told Arthur. 'Could have done with mobile phones in my day.'

'I bet.' He had so many questions, but no idea where to start. 'So the gang could keep in touch.'

Grandad nodded and settled down into the chair Arthur's father had just vacated. 'Would have saved Jonny forever running backwards and forwards with messages.' He gave a short, sharp laugh. 'I think he enjoyed it, though. Made him feel useful.' His pale eyes fixed on Arthur's. 'That's all any of us want really, to be useful.' As he spoke, he held up his gnarled, arthritic hands and stared at them. 'Not so easy to achieve these days.'

Arthur wasn't sure what to say to that, and they sat in silence for almost a minute. Somehow he was linked to the old man sitting close by. Grandad seemed to know it too – did he 'remember' Arthur's life just as Arthur could remember bits of his? Did it work both ways? Why did it work at all? But before Arthur could form a sensible question in his mind, Grandad reached under the chair and produced another newspaper.

'I think they do a crossword in here these days. Local rag,' he explained. He started to leaf through the pages, holding the paper up in front of him so he was hidden from Arthur.

'I read some old issues of that,' Arthur said. 'In

the library. They have them on microfilm, you know. There was even a review of Bessemer's Paranormal Puppet Show.'

The newspaper dropped to reveal Grandad's interested face. 'Was there now?' He smiled suddenly and leaned forward, the newspaper crumpling in his lap. 'Bet it didn't tell you everything about the show, though, did it?'

'No. I had to read something else for that.'

But Grandad seemed to have lost interest. 'Here we are.' He folded the paper so that the crossword was on the top. 'Let's see now, "Prepared to imitate the action of the tiger." What do you suppose that might be? Four and three.'

'Shakespeare, isn't it?' Arthur was not sure how he knew, but he did. '*Henry V*.' They were studying *Macbeth* in class, but that was the only Shakespeare he had ever read...

'So they do teach you something, then. I remember we did *Henry V* at school when I was your age. So the answer could be "King Hal".'

Arthur nodded thoughtfully. 'Or "copy cat",' he said.

Chapter 3

Art blamed himself. Normally, the Invisible Detective would have followed up Mr Fredericks's request for help with some questions that would make solving the case the easier. He should have asked for a better description of Tiger, when and where he was last seen, if he had any usual haunts and if he had ever gone missing before – and if so, where was he found or did he just turn up?

But with the session already ending and the audience keen to get away, Art had asked nothing. In fact, it was only because Flinch had followed the man that they even knew where he lived. So on the Wednesday evening, all other possible avenues of investigation now exhausted, Art suggested that they go and see Mr Fredericks and find out more.

'Won't he think it's odd, though?' Jonny asked. 'I mean, a few kids turning up out of the blue and quizzing him about his cat?'

'But we're working for the Invisible Detective,' Flinch said. She always had a simple answer, and Art had in fact come to a similar conclusion.

'That's right. We say we've been sent by

Brandon Lake, the Invisible Detective, to get some more details about his cat. He doesn't know there's no such person and that the Invisible Detective doesn't exist, does he?'

'But – kids?' Jonny said again.

'There's no reason why he wouldn't send children,' Meg retorted, and Jonny seemed to shrink with embarrassment. 'Sherlock Holmes used kids, didn't he, Art?'

'Yes, Meg – the Baker Street Irregulars. And you're right too, Jonny,' Art went on quickly. 'We'll have to be careful or he might become suspicious. Perhaps we shouldn't all go.'

But nobody seemed about to volunteer to be left behind, so all four of them trooped over to the courtyard off St Swithin's Lane that Flinch had described.

It was exactly as Jonny had expected from Flinch's description. The evening sun was shining on the boarded-up house beside where Mr Fredericks lived. The paintwork was faded and cracked, and most of the windows were broken. There was grass growing through the gaps between the paving slabs and a drain in the corner of the yard was blocked.

Mr Fredericks's house, by contrast, seemed well cared for and had recently been repainted. There were the remains of summer flowers in a basket hanging outside the front door. It was odd that this had not been attended to when the owner obviously took care of the rest of the house, Jonny thought. A curl of smoke seemed to hang in the air above the yard, rising from the chimney at the back of the house.

'Right,' Art said, as they all grouped round the front door, 'he's probably seen us coming anyway, so when I knock on the door, nobody run away. That means you, Jonny.'

It took Jonny a moment to realise he was joking. 'I'll be back at the den before you can say "Jack Robinson",' he told them.

Art laughed. 'I believe you.'

The sound of Art knocking on the door seemed loud in the enclosed space. It echoed off the boarded front of the next house. They waited, and after a minute Art knocked again, even louder.

But there was still no answer.

'Perhaps he's out,' Flinch said.

'The fire's lit,' Jonny pointed out. 'He won't

have gone far leaving a fire burning.'

'There's a light on in the back room as well,' Meg said. 'You can see it if you stand here.'

They all crowded round where Meg was standing, and she glared, then smiled, and moved aside.

'He's left a window open too', Flinch said. She pointed to the window on the other side of the front door.

It was on a sash, sliding sideways, and was open to the full extent though that was not very far. The gap was maybe a foot wide, maybe less. Art went to the window and cupped his hands to his mouth as he shouted through the gap: 'Hello! Mr Fredericks, are you there?' He waited for a reply, but there was none.

'Tell him the Invisible Detective sent us,' Flinch suggested.

'We don't want everyone in the neighbourhood to know,' Meg chided.

'Why not?'

'Well –'

But Art waved at them to be quiet. He was still standing at the window. As they fell into silence, Jonny could hear it too – a faint sound.

Was it an animal? A whining, keening sound. A baby perhaps.

'There's someone inside,' Art said quietly.

'Or something,' Jonny said.

'Maybe it's Tiger come home?' Flinch said.

'Perhaps he's got a wireless,' Meg suggested.

Art was considering, pacing up and down with his chin cupped in one hand. 'I don't like it,' he said at last.

'What don't you like?' Jonny asked.

'The fire's burning and a window's open.'

'The door's locked, though,' Flinch said brightly. 'I tried it just now when you were at the window.'

Art frowned, his concentration broken. 'Yes, thank you, Flinch. Anyway, I wouldn't leave a fire burning, at least not unless it was damped down or something, and there's too much smoke for that.'

'And there's the noise,' Jonny pointed out.

'And the fact that Flinch heard him being threatened,' Art went on.

'You think he's in there? Frightened to let us in?' Meg asked.

'I don't know. But let's give him another five or ten minutes, then, if there's no sign of anyone,

34

we'll take a look inside, just to be sure everything's all right.'

'And how do we get in with the door locked?' Jonny asked. He felt stupid as soon as he said it, because the answer was obvious.

'I'll go through the window and let you in,' Flinch said, grinning happily.

Art helped Flinch up to the window. By wriggling and unclicking both her shoulders, she was able to reach her arms inside the house and then turn sideways until her shoulders were also through. She smiled as she thought of Jonny's wincing when he heard the click of her joints dislocating.

She reached towards the floor, letting the joints sort themselves out before she tried to put any weight on her hands, which were now pressed into the carpet inside. The sound was louder in the house – a sort of whimpering noise that seemed to be coming from the back room. Flinch called for Art to let go of her legs and she tumbled forwards into the room.

There was no hallway, so the front door opened directly into the same room. It was not locked, but bolted, which Flinch thought meant

Mr Fredericks had gone out of the back door, wherever that led. But as she picked herself up, the whimpering noise from the back room became louder – a heart-wrenching sobbing sound. Instead of opening the front door, Flinch tiptoed across the room towards the noise.

She was scared, but also fascinated. What animal could make such a noise? At one and the same time, she was both desperate to find out and did not want to know. Just a peep, a quick look round the door, a single glance, would do no harm…

Flinch was at the door now. The wailing, sobbing, gasping sound was loud in her ears. She edged her face carefully round the doorframe, moving more and more slowly as more and more of the back room – the kitchen – became visible. The tiled floor; a large, square sink; a dark stove… She could see the edge of a large wooden chair, a shadow moving on the wall behind – flickering with the firelight. And in the chair…

They all froze at the sound of Flinch's scream. Jonny's eyes were huge as he looked at Meg. Meg's mouth was half open as she tried to speak

36

but made no sound. Art was at the door of the house in an instant, shoving uselessly at it.

Then came the sound of running feet, rapidly moving across the floor inside. The bolts scraped back and the door was flung open to reveal Flinch's face, even paler than usual beneath the ingrained dirt.

'What is it, Flinch?' Art demanded, pulling her out of the house before anything else could harm or frighten her. 'What's going on in there?'

'It's Mr Fredericks,' she said through chattering teeth. 'In the back room, the kitchen.'

'Is he all right?'

'I don't know.'

'What do you mean?' Meg asked gently, her hand trembling as she put it on Flinch's shoulder. 'What's happened to him?'

Flinch turned slowly towards Meg. 'He's got Tiger,' she said.

The cat was dead. Mr Fredericks hugged its limp form to his chest as he rocked back and forth in the chair. Flinch stood in the doorway, as if afraid to go any closer. Jonny stood with her, his hands placed reassuringly on her shoulders.

Meg and Art walked slowly towards the man. He looked up at them, but his face showed no surprise.

'Mr Fredericks?' Meg said quietly. 'It's all right, we're here to help. Is this Tiger?'

He looked down at the cat's body and, after a moment, his arms relaxed slightly and he held it out for them to see. Art gasped, glad that Flinch was not close enough for a good view.

Deep scratches and cuts ran through the animal's fur. Art could remember seeing an armchair in a neighbour's house that their new dog had ripped with its claws when they left it indoors all day. The rips in Tiger's body reminded him of that chair. But as he looked at the cuts running across Tiger's dark stripes, he knew that no dog had done this.

Mr Fredericks's whimpers were resolving themselves into speech. He was having trouble forming the words, but he was speaking now rather than just crying. 'I – I found Tiger outside,' he managed to say. 'Like this.' And he hugged the cat to his chest again.

There was a door from the kitchen, close to the sink, and Art could see that it was standing ajar. Meg pushed it open and they had a view out across a small paved yard. There was a small hut in the corner that Art assumed housed the toilet. Beyond that was an area of scrubby grass and then a broken section of wall that ran along the back of another group of houses.

'He plays out there,' Mr Fredericks explained, nodding towards the open door. 'That's where he was. Out there. Alone.'

Meg was frowning as she listened. Art knew that expression – he had seen it many times – but before he could talk to her, Mr Fredericks went on.

'He was in the storm drain.'

And in that moment, an image rose in Art's mind. The image of the bottom of a culvert, dead cats floating in the dark, scummy water. Cats that had been ripped apart…

They left Mr Fredericks with Tiger. It took only a minute to find the opening to the drain. The edge was overgrown with grass, but they could smell the sewer below and see the dark opening surrounded with crumbling bricks. It was like a small tunnel leading into the ground.

'We could climb down,' Jonny said. He did not sound enthusiastic.

'I hope that won't be necessary,' Art told him.

'Looks dark,' Flinch said, peering into the mouth of the drain. 'And it smells, that's the truth.'

'Talking of the truth,' Art said slowly, 'I saw your expression while Fredericks was speaking, Meg. Is he lying?' She would know. She always knew.

Meg was still frowning, her forehead crumpled and lined. 'I'm not sure,' she admitted. 'But like I said before, he certainly isn't telling us everything.'

'Like the creepy man who wanted Tiger,' Flinch agreed.

'He won't get the poor cat now,' Jonny said quietly.

'Is that it, do you think?' Art asked her.

'Maybe.' Meg shrugged and half smiled. 'Or it may just be that he doesn't know the truth himself. After all, he kept talking about his cat as "he".'

'People do,' Jonny told her. 'Some people actually care about their cats and dogs and pets and stuff, and call them he and she, not it.'

'Very funny,' Meg snapped back. 'And some people,' she went on, 'can tell a "he" cat from a "she" cat.'

'What do you mean?'

It was Flinch who answered. 'Tiger was a girl,' she said.

But before they could discuss this further, the middle-aged man appeared at the back door. He was still carrying the dead cat as he shuffled across the yard to join them on the grass.

'That was it,' he said. His voice seemed stronger now and his tears had dried. 'Tiger was trying to get out when I found him. Then he… he…' He broke off and turned away. After a moment he turned back, staring down into the dark tunnel.

'What can have done it?' Jonny asked. 'Do you know what killed Tiger?'

Mr Fredericks continued to stare into the drain. 'It must have been the monster,' he said, his voice husky and quiet. 'I saw it.'

They left the man standing by the tunnel, still nursing his dead Tiger. Art led them back through the house and out into the courtyard off St Swithin's Lane.

'There were dead cats in the storm drain,' Meg said. 'Where we looked before.'

'Where we found Andrew Baxter,' Jonny added. 'Remember?'

'I remember,' Art said. 'And I remember what Flinch told us he said to her.' He looked at Flinch.

Her eyes were wide as she recalled the moment. 'He said he'd seen a monster.'

Everyone at school knew Sarah Bustle. But Arthur didn't think that she knew him. Sarah was a year above him and, apart from glaring at him at the Computer Club the previous week, he was not aware that she had ever shown the slightest interest in him.

So when she came hurrying across the playground after school had finished, Arthur wondered vaguely where she was going. Perhaps, like him, she was in a rush to get home before it rained. But there was a purposefulness in her manner that suggested she was trying to catch up with someone.

She was a tall girl for fifteen. Her long black hair streamed out behind her in the breeze. Everything about Sarah Bustle was long, Arthur thought – her hair, her legs, her face. Her nose wasn't actually long as such, but it was getting close.

'Arthur – Arthur Drake!'

Her voice was long too, he decided. She drew out the vowels. He actually looked round to see who she was calling to before he realised what she had said. And even then he assumed there must be someone in her own year with the same name.

But it was obvious that she was hurrying towards him. Arthur wasn't sure whether being called by Sarah Bustle in the playground within everyone's hearing was a good thing or not. He had half a mind to run away, but he could feel his face reddening and knew he wouldn't. He was rooted to the tarmac.

'I'm glad I caught you,' she said when she reached him, slightly breathless.

'Hi,' Arthur replied. He wasn't sure what else to say.

'You're Arthur Drake, right?'

Arthur nodded.

'I saw you at Computer Club last week, though I didn't know your name.' She pushed stray strands of dark hair away from her face and tucked them behind her ear. Arthur found he was fascinated by her ear. Anything to avoid meeting her eyes. 'I don't usually go, because Squirrel knows nothing. So what's the point.'

'Er, yes,' Arthur agreed. 'Me too.'

She glanced back over her shoulder, as if worried she might be seen talking to him. 'But I thought Mr Hanshaw might be able to help me with some stuff.'

'Could he?' Arthur asked, suddenly afraid she might tire of the conversation and just leave. 'Help, I mean?'

Sarah shook her head. 'Nah. He knows more than the Squirrel. But he's still pretty useless. Anyway,' she went on quickly, 'I just wanted to ask you something.'

Arthur suppressed a shudder. 'Oh?'

'Yeah. What's your e-mail address?'

That wasn't what he expected. He didn't know what he had expected, but that wasn't it. He answered automatically, and she nodded at the gibberish stream of numbers and letters. 'It came with the computer,' he explained. 'One of those pre-installed things you get for free with the hardware. Do you want me to write it down?'

She shook her head, sending her hair spinning,

so she had to tuck it away again. 'That's all right, thanks.' She seemed preoccupied, almost as if she wasn't really interested in the answer at all. As if he was telling her something she already knew. She turned away without another word.

'Nice talking to you,' Arthur said sarcastically. He didn't intend her to hear.

But she turned and for some reason she was smiling – a huge face-changing smile that shortened her features somehow and for a moment made him forget everything else. 'Nice talking to you too,' she said. 'See you, then.' Her long legs were already taking her across the playground. Arthur watched her as far as the gate. Then his attention was caught by someone else.

It was his dad, hurrying across the playground. It surprised him that Sarah Bustle stepped politely out of Dad's way. It surprised him that Dad was here at all. It surprised him to find that he was running towards Dad to meet him halfway – to discover why he looked so drawn, so pale, so worried.

'Dad, what is it? I wasn't expecting you. You don't usually come and meet me.'

'It's Grandad,' his father said. His voice was as

strained and anxious as his expression.

'Is he all right?'

'How did he seem to you the other day?' Dad was leading him out of the playground. 'You spent more time talking to him than I did. Did he seem... OK?'

Arthur could feel his stomach was churning. 'Fine. He was in fine form. Same as ever. Why? What's happened, Dad? Is Gramps all right?' He was an old man, Arthur was telling himself. But he'd seemed so full of life. 'Has he – I mean, is he...' He didn't know how to say it.

But Dad understood. 'No,' he said quickly. 'At least, I hope not.'

'What, then?'

'He's gone,' Dad said simply. 'Disappeared.'

Chapter 4

The Baxters lived the other side of the Monument. Art and Jonny knocked on the door after school the next day.

'He plays football, remember?' Art said as they waited. He could hear someone moving about in the hallway, and a moment later there was the sound of a bolt being pulled back.

The woman who opened the door had greying hair tied in a bun and was wearing an apron. She wiped her hands on it as she regarded the two boys with suspicion. Art could see that there was flour on her hands. Her face was red, the skin slack, so that she looked like an over ripe apple.

'I'm not buying anything,' she told them, and made to close the door again.

'We're not selling anything,' Art replied quickly. 'We were looking for Andrew. He'd said he'd come out and play football after school.'

The door paused. 'You've just missed him,' she said, without looking. 'He got tired of waiting, I expect.'

'Do you know where he went?' Jonny asked politely.

'To the yard, maybe,' Art suggested, remembering where they had learned he liked to kick a ball about, and where he had fallen off the wall and into a culvert.

The door swung open again. 'No, he has not,' Andrew's mother told them emphatically. 'I don't know where he's gone, but I've told him he's never to go back there. So's his father. Not after what happened...' She took a deep breath and seemed to calm a little. 'You know about that, I suppose?'

Art nodded, keen not to get a descriptive lecture on the dangers of climbing walls and hanging around in secluded yards close to the river. 'He told us. Thanks. We'll find him.'

The woman's eyes narrowed and she closed the door slowly, as if waiting for Art to add something further. But Art said nothing until it was closed and bolted again.

'He's gone to the yard,' he said to Jonny.

Jonny nodded. 'Sure to have done.'

They could hear the ball hitting the wall and bouncing off before they could see into the yard. Andrew was alone, kicking the ball into the corner and letting it bounce back at random from the uneven walls. He did not see them until the ball got past him and he had to turn and run after it.

Jonny got there first, trapping the leather football under his shoe, then rolling it back across the cobbled ground.

'Thanks.' The fair-haired boy helped the ball on its way towards the wall. Then he paused and looked more closely at Jonny and Art. 'Hey – it's you,' he said.

'Could be,' Art agreed with a grin.

'What are you doing here?' He turned towards the wall once more, waiting for the ball to return, poised to hammer it back again.

'Looking for you,' Jonny said. He glanced at Art, the faintest trace of a smile on his lips. 'Your mum sent us.'

Andrew was in mid-kick as Jonny said this. He missed the ball completely and had to stagger to retain his balance. His face was full of alarm, and even his freckles seemed drained of colour.

Art laughed. 'Don't worry. She said you wouldn't be here, so of course we guessed you were.'

Andrew laughed too. But he still looked and sounded nervous. 'Oh, right,' he said. 'Joke. I get it.'

'Joke,' Jonny agreed.

'So, what do you want?' His face was getting some colour back now.

'We wanted to ask you about the monster.'

Andrew went white again. He sat down on the ground and hugged his knees to his chest. Art went and sat beside him. The cobbles were uneven and they were so cold that they felt damp through his trousers.

'I think it was just a dream,' Andrew said quietly. 'I was so frightened, you know? Stuck down there for days. I thought I'd had it, that no one would ever find me. I couldn't sleep at first, and my leg hurt so much…' He stared off into the furthest corner of the yard as he remembered the ordeal. 'But I think I dozed off. Must have done. There was a dead cat. Maybe more than one. At first I thought it was moving, purring in the darkness or something.' He shrugged. 'Just a dream.'

'Tell us anyway,' Art said gently. 'Tell us what you dreamed.'

'I dreamed a monster came. That's all. I couldn't really see it, of course. The moon shone in a bit, so I could see fur and teeth.' He shuddered. 'Lots of teeth. Big teeth. And it smelled of my aunt's coat when she comes in from the rain. It rubbed against me, brushed my face. I had to bite my lip not to make a noise. Then it went.' He jumped to his feet and ran to kick the ball again.

'Where did it go?' Jonny asked him. 'In your dream?'

The ball hit the wall and arced back towards Andrew. He volleyed it at the brickwork once more. 'It just went. Couldn't climb out, so it must have gone back down the tunnel. It sloped away, into the sewer, I s'pose.' He hammered the ball again, miskicking it so it caught the top of his shoe and span lazily up into the air to bounce just a few yards away. 'Yeah,' he decided. 'That's where it went. Whatever it really was.'

'I'm afraid that Mr Fredericks could not be with us again this evening,' the Invisible Detective told the people gathered in the dimly lit upstairs room. 'You will recall that he was concerned about his cat and sadly the news is not good.' There was a lot of shuffling of feet, suggesting that the fate of Mr Fredericks's cat was not of terrific interest to everyone.

Jonny watched proceedings from behind the curtain. He was holding a fishing rod, ready to lower any message that might be needed to Art in the armchair. There was not enough light in the room for anyone to see the line play out. Meg and Flinch were standing further along in the area between the curtain and the bay window.

Beyond the curtains the fidgeting had subsided and there was now the sort of expectant hush that descends when people expect bad news. 'Tiger was found dead, close to Mr Fredericks's house. I am afraid I can tell you no more now, but investigations are proceeding.'

Someone coughed at the back of the room and the detective paused. 'Can I ask,' a husky voiced enquired, 'if there is more to this than meets the eye, as they say? I mean, why are you wasting your time with a dead cat, for goodness' sake? Or is it all part of the same case?'

Jonny looked at Meg, wondering if she knew what the man meant. She shrugged and shook her head. Flinch was looking out of the window, down into Cannon Street below.

Art's disguised voice answered after a short pause. 'Let us just say that I have told you as much as I am able to at the moment,' he said slowly. 'But if anyone has anything to offer that might help with these further investigations I mentioned...' He let the question hang like the fishing line in the air.

'Well,' the husky man said, 'it's just that with so many cats missing... And all this talk of mutilation and torn-up cats' bodies and birds and even that dog in the blocked drain in Badger's Passage...'

Another voice joined in from the other side of the room. Jonny leaned out in an effort to see the woman who was talking now, his head brushing against Meg's curls as she did the same. 'What about them rats?'

'Er, rats?' the Invisible Detective asked, momentarily caught off guard. His voice sounded slightly higher-pitched than usual, but the woman continued without appearing to notice.

'Overran that house in St Swithin's Lane, they did. You must've heard of that.'

'Ah.' The detective's mellow tones were restored now. '*Those* rats.'

'Coming up out of the sink, they were. And the drains. Poor Mrs Briggson didn't know what to do. Chased 'em with a broom, she did, till there were too many to cope with. Then she ran screaming to the gasworks for her husband to come home and sort it out.'

'Did he sort it?' someone asked.

'Him? Not likely. Refused to go back home with her, so she had to find a copper. Then, when they got there, the rats had all gone. The copper wanted to know if she'd been drinking, she said. The cheek of it.'

'And had she been drinking?' another voice wondered.

The Invisible Detective cut in loudly before this could spark any further discussion. 'As I said, investigations are continuing.' There was silence again, an expectant silence. Jonny could tell that they were waiting for something more, and after a pause they got it as Art seemed to realise this too. 'These investigations do, of course, include the rat incident at Mrs Briggson's in St Swithin's Lane.'

'And what investigation is this about rats and Mrs Briggson?' Meg demanded as soon as the audience had gone and they were alone again.

'It sounds like the events are connected,'

Art told her.

'I don't see why.'

'Coincidence?' Jonny offered, as he counted the coins left by people who had asked questions. 'I mean, there's been a bank robbery as well as dead cats, but there's no connection there.'

'I suppose not,' Art conceded. 'But it would do no harm to make sure.'

Meg watched him closely, her arms folded and eyes narrow. 'And how do we do that?'

'Go to the police?' Jonny said. He meant Art's dad, and they all knew it.

'They ain't interested,' Flinch told him. 'That woman said.' She gave a shrug. 'It's only rats.'

'Who, then?'

'Maybe we could ask Charlie,' Flinch said.

Charlie joined the Cannoniers for tea and fruitcake on a Tuesday afternoon at the tearoom on the concourse at Cannon Street station when he was free. This was actually not very often – perhaps only once every three weeks. He was a busy man, though none of them knew exactly what he did. But he was their friend and had helped them before, when they needed someone to act as a messenger for the Invisible Detective. All of the Cannoniers trusted and respected the elderly white-haired man, and he in turn admired and trusted them.

This week they were lucky, and Charlie met them in their warehouse den at five o'clock, before walking with them to the station. Over tea, Art explained what they had learned about the rats. As ever, Charlie listened attentively. His mass of white hair seemed to have a life of its own, shimmering and dancing with the slightest movement of his head. His watery pale eyes were fixed on Art as he told his story.

'Rats have been a problem in London for centuries,' Charlie said when Art had finished. 'A problem that comes and goes. It may depend on the weather, on how high the river is, any number of things.' His face cracked as he smiled. 'I doubt it's anything to do with some mysterious monster.'

'You don't think there's a monster?' Jonny asked.

'Do you? Can you really put your hand on your heart and say, "Yes, I believe that there's a monster running around London, killing the cats and frightening the rats, but only one distraught man and an exhausted boy have seen it?"'

'It does seem a little far-fetched,' Art conceded. Listening to his own description of events, he had been struck by how thin and silly it all sounded.

'But what if there really *is* a monster?' Flinch demanded, helping herself to another slice of cake.

'There isn't,' Meg told her shortly. 'That's what Charlie's saying.'

'I'm saying it's extremely unlikely,' Charlie agreed. 'So I shouldn't go chasing after it. Because either you're wasting your time or…' He let his voice trail off.

'Or what?' Jonny asked.

'Well,' Charlie said, 'I don't think it would be a very good idea to go chasing *real* monsters, do you?'

'You think Mr Fredericks imagined it?' Art asked. 'And Andrew Baxter too?'

'The boy's not really sure what he saw,' Meg said. 'If anything. And Mr Fredericks is in a state because of his poor cat.'

'Tiger,' Flinch reminded them.

'Yes, Tiger.'

'Cats get killed every day, more's the pity,' Charlie said, draining his tea and standing up. 'They get killed by other animals – foxes, even. Run over by cars or trains. Meet with all sorts of accidents.' He retrieved his coat from a stand beside the table and pulled it on. 'It's hardly unusual, I'm afraid.'

'I'm beginning to think you're right,' Art said. 'We got carried along because the poor man was so worked up about it, that's all.'

'You'll have to excuse me, I'm afraid, but I have guests this evening. Weathers will get nervous if I'm not home soon.'

Art could not imagine Charlie's calm and refined butler, Weathers, getting nervous about anything. War could break out, but he would merely nod as if he had expected it and suggest that the curtains should be drawn. They said their goodbyes, and Charlie promised to try to see them next Tuesday before paying for the tea and cake.

'So that's it, then,' Jonny said, when the old man had left them. 'Nothing to investigate, nothing to report back.' His disappointment was obvious.

'Seems that way.' Art tried to keep his own disappointment out of his voice.

'What about Mr Fredericks?' Meg asked.

'Like you said, he was upset about his cat. You can imagine all sorts of things when you're in that frame of mind.'

'That's not what I meant.' She was looking at Art the way she did when he was supposed to understand what she was on about. He didn't, and she knew it. 'I'm still not convinced he was telling us everything. And anyway, we can't just abandon him,' she explained, as if to a three-year-old. 'He's in no fit state to look after himself.'

'He'll get over it,' Jonny said.

'But until he does, I think we should look after him.'

'Nurse Meg?' Art said with a smile.

'She's right,' Flinch said. 'Poor man.'

'I just mean we should check he's all right now and again. Take him some food, not spoon-feed it to him. Until he's over the shock.'

'It was only a cat,' Jonny muttered. But then he caught Flinch's expression and turned away with a sigh. 'Sorry.'

'OK, OK,' Art said. 'We'll keep an eye on him for a couple of days, just to make sure he's over the loss of Tiger. All right?' He looked round at his friends, all watching him now, serious. 'But I don't think we need to go overboard about it. One of us can call each day to ask how he is. And we'll keep watch on his house when we can to make sure he seems all right.'

Flinch grinned at this and Meg nodded. Jonny raised his eyebrows but said nothing.

On the way back to the den, Art made sure that he and Jonny lagged slightly behind the girls.

'Are we really going to keep watch on some geezer who's weeping over his moggie?' Jonny asked.

'Of course,' Art said. He almost laughed at Jonny's expression. 'Meg's right, we ought to make sure he can cope. He was pretty upset, remember?'

Jonny grunted. He did not sound amused.

'But there's another reason,' Art said quietly.

Jonny looked up, his eyes wide with expectation. 'What?'

'Meg thought he was lying about something. Or, at least, not telling us the whole truth.'

Jonny nodded. 'That's right.'

'It's probably nothing important. But even so,' Art said, 'I'd like to know what it is.'

* * *

Since it was Meg's idea, it was agreed that she should be the first to visit Mr Fredericks. If it turned out that he had made a full recovery, then Meg could simply convey the Cannoniers' sympathy and leave. But if he was still shaken up by his ordeal, then she would offer help and see if he needed food or milk or anything collecting.

Meg felt a pang of guilt as she approached St Swithin's Lane. She had taken two bread rolls from the pantry, wrapping them in a clean handkerchief. She knew her mother could not really afford to give food away, but Meg felt more guilty that she had taken them for someone other than Flinch. If she took food from the house for anyone apart from herself, it was always for Flinch. But as she turned into the tiny courtyard and saw the boarded-up house opposite where Mr Fredericks lived, her doubts faded and she knew she was here to help.

It was strangely quiet in the yard. The traffic on Cannon Street was a distant murmur. A taxi cut down St Swithin's Lane, its wheels clattering on the cobbles. But the sounds of London seemed to recede as the taxi faded away.

Meg did not have much time. She wanted to

be home before her father. He would probably not be back until late, until after they threw him out of the pub at closing time. She did not want to see him, but she did want to be there with her mother when he arrived. She hesitated outside the house, wondering what to say to Mr Fredericks. Would he be grateful for the bread or embarrassed? Would he even remember who she was or understand why she had come? Should she perhaps simply leave the handkerchief of bread on the doorstep, knock and leave?

As she considered, Meg became aware of a murmuring sound. It was distinct from the distant rumble of the traffic. Closer. It was coming from the open window beside the door in front of her. People talking in raised voices.

Almost instinctively, Meg strained to hear. She leaned towards the window on tiptoes, carefully avoiding the broken drain cover that was set in the corner of the yard and overgrown with something green and unpleasant. One of the voices, she was sure, belonged to Mr Fredericks, and he sounded angry. The other was louder, closer and even angrier.

'...they were still unstable,' it sounded like

Mr Fredericks was saying.

'You haven't left us much choice,' the other man retorted angrily. 'Your greedy scheme has endangered everything. *People*,' he said significantly, 'are not pleased.'

Mr Fredericks's reply was too quiet for Meg to catch, but she heard the other man easily enough.

'But it did, didn't it? And now we have to retrieve the –' he paused, as if searching for the right word – 'situation. Twenty-four hours, and that's it,' the angry voice continued. 'This time tomorrow, if you haven't retrieved it, we'll send in another one to sniff it out.'

'I thought you said they were unstable,' Mr Fredericks protested, his voice a nasal whine.

'I don't think you've left us much choice,' the other man snapped back. 'One day, that's all.' There were heavy footsteps heading towards the door as the man spoke and his voice was getting louder as he approached. 'And you'd better pray that you find it.'

Mr Fredericks was saying something, but Meg did not try to catch what it was. She had no idea who the other man was, but she knew she didn't want him to find her outside the door or guess she might have overheard. She ran to the yard's entrance and out into the lane beyond. Once there, she ducked into a doorway shadowed from the sun by the high buildings opposite.

A few moments later a tall, thin man stepped out into the lane. He wore a top hat and carried a silver-topped cane. The collar of his dark-grey coat was turned up so that Meg could see almost nothing of his face. He glanced along the lane towards where Meg was hiding and she shrank back, pressing herself against the door behind her. But the man turned quickly in the opposite direction and strode away. Meg could see the anger still in his steps, could imagine the dark fury on his face as he reached the end of the lane and disappeared into Cannon Street beyond.

Grandad's room seemed the best place to start. Arthur sat on the bed, trying to think what might have happened to the old man, while Dad questioned the staff.

Arthur spent some time leafing through papers on the bedside cabinet in the hope that his grandfather might have left a note or a clue to explain where he had gone. But there was nothing – a postcard from a friend, a leaflet advertising digital hearing aids, and a form to donate money to a charity, together with a prepaid reply envelope. Apart from the cabinet, the rest of the room was ordered, neat and tidy – no papers or books or clutter on display. All was meticulously clear and clean and dusted.

Arthur considered checking the little desk that stood against the wall. But he decided it must be locked, and anyway that would have seemed like an intrusion. He felt bad enough just looking at the papers on the cabinet – going through his grandad's desk would be unbearable.

Dad returned after about half an hour. His expression immediately told Arthur that he had learned nothing useful.

'Someone saw him going out into the garden mid-morning, about eleven,' Dad said glumly. 'He wasn't in his room when they came to tell him lunch was ready and he wasn't in the garden either.'

'Doesn't he have to sign out or something?'

Arthur wondered. Visitors had to sign in.

'This isn't a prison, you know,' Dad said quickly. It was an automatic answer, and he rubbed his eyes and forehead afterwards. He sat down next to Arthur on the bed. 'Sorry. No, but most of the people here don't go out without telling anyone. A lot of them aren't up to it anyway.' Dad stood up again, pacing the room in agitation. 'Where would he go? He's never done this before. Never. They just thought he'd gone for a walk, or to buy a paper. He does sometimes.'

'But not this time,' Arthur said.

'And he never misses his meals. You know what he's like for punctuality.'

Arthur didn't, but he let his dad go on pacing and talking. 'I've rung the hospitals. Nothing. I rang the local station to...'

'You think he caught a train?'

'*Police* station.'

'Of course.'

Dad stopped pacing and turned to face Arthur. 'He didn't say anything yesterday? When you were with him? Anything at all that might tell us where he's gone?'

'You were here too,' Arthur reminded him.

'Well, except when you took that call.'

'What did you talk about then?'

Arthur paused. He didn't want to lie to his father. But equally, he wasn't ready to tell him the truth. We talked about how I can sometimes remember parts of his life as if it's my own, he didn't say. About how he used to know the weird things that I know. About a stone that the old man in the antiques shop on Cannon Street gave me and when you look into it you can sort of see the past. About how Grandad is Art, and Art is the Invisible Detective...

Instead he replied, 'We did the crossword in the local paper.'

Somehow, the memory of the two of them sitting together on the same bed, huddled over the folded newspaper, brought home to Arthur how sad he was. He had just started to get to know his grandfather – just started to realise what they had in common. Just decided that he had someone he could talk to after all about the strange things he was experiencing – dreams and thoughts and memories... Now he was gone. Snatched away and as invisible as Brandon Lake himself.

As much to hide the tears welling up as

anything else, Arthur bent forward and pulled the metal waste bin from under the bedside cabinet. There was the newspaper, still folded to the crossword, dropped into the bin. He pulled it out and stared through blurred eyes at the chequer-board pattern with confident capital letters printed darkly in the white squares. He had after all settled on COPY CAT, Arthur saw with a sad smile.

A thin strip of paper fluttered down to land at Arthur's feet. It had fallen from the newspaper, he realised, as he bent to pick it up and dropped it into the bin. But why, he thought – why now? Why hadn't it fallen out yesterday, when they were doing the crossword? Unless…

Carefully, cautiously, Arthur opened out the paper and started to turn back through the pages.

'What are you doing?'

He continued his slow progress through the paper, passing the estate agents' supplement and moving back into local news. Suddenly, there it was. Arthur held the page up for his father to see, looking at him through the hole. A rectangle of paper had been removed from one side of the page, and the strip that had fallen out was the discarded margin.

'He cut something out of the paper,' Arthur's

father said slowly.

'It's not on the bedside cabinet. So unless it's in his desk…'

Arthur's dad had fewer qualms about checking the desk than Arthur had. The top folded down and it wasn't locked. Inside was ordered and neat – papers arranged in tidy piles and folded into pigeonholes. One of the drawers was locked, but Dad found the key in a compartment in the top section. Inside the drawer was an album of sepia photographs. Dad leafed quickly through it, and Arthur caught brief awkward glimpses of people and places as they turned past.

Behind the photo album was a cardboard box about the size of a shoebox. It was tied with discoloured string and they could both tell that the knot was old. Nowhere did they find a recent news clipping.

'Perhaps he gave it away to someone.' Dad checked the bin again. 'It's not in here. I wonder what it was about.'

'Perhaps he took it with him,' Arthur said, speaking both their minds. 'Perhaps it's why he's gone.'

Chapter 5

Jonny was all for going round and quizzing Mr Fredericks there and then. He seemed determined to find some reason for continuing the Cannoniers' investigations and Meg's account of what she had heard was enough for him.

The others were less determined. Meg was not sure what she had heard – implied threats and angry words. But they could relate to anything. Perhaps, she suggested, Mr Fredericks owed the other man some money. Flinch was still concerned about Tiger and how Mr Fredericks was coping with the loss of his cat. She sat on a roll of carpet and gnawed at one of the bread rolls Meg had brought.

As was so often the case, it was left to Art to decide on a course of action. 'There's still something here that doesn't add up,' he decided, tapping his finger against his chin as he thought. 'As Meg says, the business with the other man may be unrelated, but we still haven't solved the mystery of the monster and there are no other leads.'

'And maybe no monster,' Meg reminded him.

'That's what Charlie said.'

'He's probably right,' Art admitted.

'So are we just going to drop it?' Jonny wanted to know. 'The Invisible Detective admits defeat?'

Art knew he was saying this just to get a reaction. 'The Invisible Detective never admits defeat,' he replied. Jonny failed to stifle a grin of satisfaction. 'Though it's hardly a defeat to report that there is actually no mystery. But don't worry,' he went on, as Jonny frowned, 'we aren't dropping it yet. Not until we're absolutely certain there's nothing more to investigate.'

'And how do we make certain?' Jonny asked.

'We'll talk to Mr Fredericks again. But not tonight. It's getting late and I know Meg needs to get home.' She smiled briefly at this, then looked away. Flinch was yawning. Art went on, 'Tomorrow morning, I'll look in on my way to school and just ask him if everything's all right now. It's on my way.'

'It's on my way too,' Meg said quickly. 'Or nearly.'

'All right.' Art nodded. 'But just the two of us, I think. He's more likely to talk to fewer people and Meg will know if he's being less than honest.'

Flinch and Jonny seemed happy with this, and after a few more minutes the others left Flinch to get some sleep. Meg checked she was snuggled into the 'nest' she had made from pieces of old carpet and a couple of blankets, then they let themselves out of the disused warehouse and made their separate ways home through the thickening evening.

Meg was already waiting at the corner of Cannon Street and St Swithin's Lane when Art arrived. He had slept longer than he intended and had dreamed about the monster. Or rather, he had dreamed that he was reading newspaper reports about the monster. The dream was so vivid and real that when he woke up it took him several moments to realise it had been a dream at all.

'Sorry,' he gasped as he ran up. 'Overslept.'

Meg said nothing. She was holding a folded handkerchief and when Art stared at it she unwrapped it enough to reveal a bread roll inside.

'Good idea.' said Art, wishing he had thought of bringing some food or something as an excuse for calling.

Mr Fredericks opened the door before they even knocked on it. It was as if he had been waiting for them. He seemed agitated and looked as if he had not slept. His hair was all over the place and there were dark patches below his eyes.

'Oh, it's you,' he said, as he stepped back and ushered them inside. He glanced at the bread roll Meg was offering without seeming to realise it was meant for him. 'The Invisible Detective,' he said urgently, 'has he found the monster yet?'

Art and Meg exchanged glances. He must still be very upset about his cat, Art thought, to be so keen for the monster to be found. Was he worried about other cats and pets, or was he looking for justice for his own loss?

'He's still making enquiries,' Art said, as they stood in the front room. 'He sent us to see if you were all right.'

This seemed to surprise Mr Fredericks. He stood rubbing his hands together without saying anything.

'And to ask you a few things.'

He seemed to brighten slightly at this, and Meg again offered the bread roll.

'We brought you something to eat,' she said.

'You have to eat, to keep your strength up. Can we sit down?'

She sat carefully on the ragged sofa without waiting for an answer and, following her cue, Mr Fredericks sat next to her.

Art sank into the armchair, finding the springs had gone and disappearing further into it than he had expected. 'About Tiger,' he said, hauling himself back to perch on the edge of the chair. 'You found him close to the storm drain, that's right, isn't it?'

Mr Fredericks nodded. He was holding the bread roll, but he made no attempt to take a bite. Art had skipped breakfast, he was so late, and the sight and smell of the fresh bread was making his stomach churn with interest.

'Tiger was just lying there.' The man suppressed his emotions and looked away.

Art could see the side of his mouth crease into what he assumed was a stifled sob.

Meg put her hand gently on Mr Fredericks's arm. 'It's all right,' she said. 'You've told us already.' She shot a look at Art, obviously wanting him to stop this line of questioning.

'So tell us about the monster,' Art said. He

intended it to be matter-of-fact, but to him at least it just sounded ridiculous.

The effect on Mr Fredericks, however, was startling. He immediately seemed to become more interested and animated. 'It was here,' he gasped. 'That night.'

'Out by the storm drain?' Art wanted to know. 'Or actually in the drain?' If it was *in* the drain, then Mr Fredericks could have seen anything – murky water swilling about in the moonlight; shadows; another cat even. Anything.

But Mr Fredericks was shaking his head. 'No, not outside.' His eyes were wide with the memory as he turned his tear-stained face towards Art. 'Here,' he repeated. 'This is where it attacked me. Right here. In the house.'

Jonny took over from Meg at just after nine o'clock. She had said she was happy to stay with Flinch until half-past, but Jonny knew she would want to be home before her dad got in from the pub, so he made sure he was early. He ran all the way, delighting in the feel of the cold evening air rushing through his hair. The lamp-lit pavement was a blur beneath his feet and Jonny hummed a happy tune, although even he could not hear it for the sound of the breeze as he raced across London.

He found Meg and Flinch sitting on a broken section of low wall at the edge the waste ground behind Mr Fredericks's house. The wall ran along the back gardens of another row of houses, and Jonny could see the girls silhouetted against the greying sky. They looked like statues huddled together in the gathering chill of the evening.

They had a good view of the back of the place, although the nearest and most prominent bit of Mr Fredericks's home was the outside toilet in the corner of the yard, its square wooden form jutting up above the back wall. The boards were rotting and the light from the kitchen beyond was visible through the gaps.

'Tea didn't take long,' Jonny said, hoping Meg wouldn't realise why he had really come early. He handed Flinch a brown paper bag in which he had slipped a couple of scones. 'Anything exciting happened?'

When they met that afternoon, the Cannoniers had agreed to keep watch on Mr Fredericks's house for a couple of nights in case the monster should return. Meg was adamant that there was a monster – or at least that Mr Fredericks really believed there was. She was still insistent that they should do all they could to look after the man until he was fully recovered from his ordeal.

Art seemed less convinced, but he was certain that something strange was going on and they should find out what. His father was on duty that night, so he was due to slip out and relieve Jonny at eleven o'clock. Jonny's parents were happy for him to be out late with his friends, though if they saw him sneaking back in after about eleven at the latest he would have some explaining to do.

'Nothing going on at all,' Meg said as Flinch munched appreciatively on a scone. 'Mr Fredericks is in there. He went out earlier, but he's back now. Cooked his tea a little while ago.'

'Went to the toilet,' Flinch added, spraying bits of scone. Not that Jonny needed or wanted to know that. 'Then he went upstairs. Gone to bed early, I think.'

'If you want to leave,' Jonny said to Meg, 'we'll manage.'

Meg rarely smiled. But Jonny recognised the way her mouth twitched as a close equivalent. 'I will, if you don't mind,' she said. 'Mum's expecting me.'

They sat in silence for a while after Meg had left. Flinch finished her scones, shaking a last few crumbs out of the bag. 'Thanks, Jonny.'

'My pleasure.' They were sitting on the wall. Jonny could feel the cold seeping through the seat of his trousers. Flinch was swinging her legs and humming quietly. He didn't recognise the tune and suspected she had made it up. She was wearing a threadbare coat that used to belong to Meg.

'Have you read Art's casebook?' Flinch asked after a while. The moon was shining brightly down, unworried by the fragile clouds that skimmed its surface. 'I mean,' she went on, 'you can read and all.'

'I can read,' he answered, smiling. 'But Art keeps that book to himself. It's just notes, I expect. Thoughts. Lists of suspects and stuff.'

'That's what I think.' She continued to swing her legs and hummed some more. 'Is he all right? Art, I mean.'

The question surprised Jonny. 'I think so. What do you mean?'

Flinch shrugged and huddled closer to Jonny in the chill air. 'I dunno,' she confessed. 'But he says strange things sometimes. And I did think maybe he was cross still that we knew about his dad being a copper.'

'He didn't mind. He just didn't realise we knew. So it was a shock. He does say strange things,' Jonny went on. 'Something about wishing he had a telephone you could carry round with you the other day.' Jonny laughed as he remembered. 'But that's because – well, because he's Art, I suppose.'

Flinch nodded. 'S'pose so.' Suddenly she stiffened, becoming alert. 'What's that noise?'

Jonny strained to hear, but the breeze and the distant traffic and the sounds of the city obscured everything else. He shook his head. 'You humming, probably.'

Flinch held up her hand. 'No, it's more squeaky than that. Listen.'

He listened, but he still couldn't hear anything unusual. 'Where's it coming from? Which direction?'

'From the house, I think.'

Jonny pushed himself off the low wall, then turned to help Flinch down. 'Let's go and see.' He grinned at her in the moonlight. 'It could be a squeaky monster.' He laughed as her eyes widened. 'Only joking.'

They were almost at the back yard of Mr Fredericks's house before Jonny could hear what Flinch meant. She was right, it was a squeaking sound – like a hundred badly oiled gates all swinging together in the wind.

'What is it?' Jonny wondered out loud.

'It's coming from the toilet,' Flinch said. She looked worried and Jonny could see that she was shivering. 'I don't want to look.'

'All right,' he reassured her, though he was apprehensive himself now. 'I'll look. We won't open the door. It's just something that needs oiling, I expect.'

Cautiously, they tiptoed up to the wooden hut. The door was closed, held shut with a stub of wood screwed to the doorframe that twisted over the door itself to stop it swinging open. There was probably a bolt on the inside, Jonny thought. As they got closer, he could see that the door was moving, rattling against the wooden latch. The wind, he told himself, it must be the wind. But the breeze had died and the air was still.

'Wait here.' Jonny left Flinch in the yard, halfway between the toilet shed and the back door of the house. 'Run to the kitchen if there's trouble and get Mr Fredericks. All right?'

Flinch nodded quickly, biting her lower lip.

Jonny sidled up to the shed, leaning cautiously towards the side, nervous of touching the wooden wall. He angled his head so he could peer through a narrow gap between two of the boards. There was enough moonlight seeping into the shed for him to make out the opposite wall. The door was rattling more fiercely now. He moved slightly and he could see a wad of paper attached to the wall by a string run through the corners. Further still and he could see the grubby white of the lavatory bowl. Still the door fought against the latch.

But Jonny did not hear it. His attention was entirely on what he could see. On the lavatory, the dark interior, the shapes moving round inside the shed. They were scrabbling across the ground so that the floor seemed to be alive, they were inside the toilet itself, making the water seethe and writhe.

Suddenly one of them detached itself from the mass and leaped out of the water. It slammed into the wooden wall close to the gap where Jonny was looking in. Cold, scummy water splashed into his face and he blinked. Scrabbling on the wood now, claws rattling across the other side of the wall, as Jonny leaped back and stifled a cry that was a mixture of surprise, disgust, fear and horror.

Then he turned and ran for the house, grabbing Flinch's hand as he reached her and dragging the girl after him.

'What is it?' she gasped. 'What's in there?

He tore open the kitchen door and flung himself inside, still holding tight to Flinch's hand. 'Rats! Hundreds of them.'

They both froze. Jonny's words could just as easily have been a description of the inside of the kitchen. There were rats everywhere. The floor was a carpet of the creatures, long, scaled tails flicking across each other's slimy backs as they jostled and fought. The sink was overflowing with the creatures, their dark eyes picking up the moonlight and shining in the gloom. There were so many it was impossible to tell where one of them ended and another began. And they seemed to move as one creature – towards Jonny and Flinch.

At first it was their heads, turning towards the opening door and the sound of Jonny's voice. Their squeals and shrieks died away for a few seconds as if they were assessing the situation. Then one of the rats leaped from the counter next to the sink, flying across the room towards Flinch.

She screamed as the slicked, wet animal hurtled towards her – towards her face. Jonny let go of her hand and lashed out, catching the rat in the side as it passed, knocking it to the floor. He could hear it screeching in outrage, as if it was calling on the other rats to take up its fight.

Flinch backed away, shaking so much Jonny was afraid she would collapse. He took her hand again and pulled her back through the door, away from the mass of fur and claws that seemed to be gathering itself for an attack. As soon as they were in the yard, Jonny slammed the door shut.

But it closed on a sudden rush of the creatures, jamming against their bodies. He tried to force it shut, felt the door give, felt tiny bones crunch. But first a few, then more and more, of the animals were forcing their way out through the narrow gap. The trickle became a stream – became a torrent of the dripping, slimy animals. When he felt one land on his leg, felt the claws scrabble at his trousers, imagined the sharp white teeth preparing to strike, Jonny gave up and let go of the door.

Together they turned and ran. There were rats under their feet, sending them tripping and skidding across the yard. The moon watched impassively as they staggered as fast as they could for the opening out into the wasteland. Almost level with the toilet now…

The door of the little hut was rattling more than ever. The sound was like thunder beneath the shriek of the attacking rats. But part of that shriek, Jonny realised, was tearing wood as the latch was ripped from its screw and the door exploded outwards. He tightened his grip on Flinch's hand and dragged her even faster across the yard.

The rats seemed to fall out of the hut, as if they had been stacked up high against the door. They hurled themselves out over the cobbles and after Jonny and Flinch. The wasteland – almost at the wasteland. If they could get back to the broken wall, they could at least get above the creatures.

Somewhere across the river, the first of London's clocks started to strike the hour. Ten o'clock. And the wall was a lifetime away. Flinch was gasping, staggering, almost fell. Jonny could outrun the rats, he could outrun anything. But he had to keep hold of Flinch.

Her hand was torn from his grasp as she fell. He was going so fast that Jonny took yards to stop, precious seconds to turn and run back. By the time he had helped Flinch back to her feet, the rats were on them. Flinch was screaming, Jonny was hammering at the dark shapes with his fists, shuddering at the squelch and squeal, ignoring the scratches and tears at his hands. Kicking at anything that moved. Over Flinch's shoulder, as he knocked a rat from its perch there, he could see the whole of the area of wasteland was now a sea of slippery movement.

Almost the whole of it. There was one ragged hole in the scratching, biting, screeching nightmare. One chance. Flinch had seen it too.

'The storm drain,' she shouted.

'Rats live in drains,' he screamed back at her.

But already they were running, hardly daring to think what their feet were trampling as they scrambled across the moving landscape towards the black mouth of the drain.

'They're leaving the drains,' Flinch shouted back. 'Why, Jonny?'

He didn't know, didn't care. There was no time to worry about it now.

Something swiped viciously across Jonny's cheek and he shrieked as loud and clear as the rats around them. He swiped his hand across the pain and felt it connect with something wet and warm and unpleasant. Only a few yards now.

They leaped together. How deep was it, he tried to remember? How far to fall? How much water in the bottom?

Or perhaps, he thought, as they fell together and it was too late to change their minds, it was not water in the drain at all. Perhaps a black mass of fur and malevolence was waiting down there for them – with outstretched claws and bared teeth...

There was a new edition of the paper at the newsagent's. It was published weekly, and the edition in Grandad's waste bin was ten days old.

'Don't you have any of last week's left?' Arthur asked in exasperation. He had gone half a mile out of his way after school. The newsagent shook his head and Arthur silently cursed himself for not thinking of coming the previous day. 'It sold out?'

The newsagent was a small man with a thin attempt at a moustache which twitched as he laughed. 'I wish,' he said. 'No, they take last week's away when they bring the new edition. What's wrong with this week's anyway?'

'What do they do with the old papers?' Arthur wondered.

The little man shrugged. 'Pulp them probably. Or shred them.' He went back to working through a set of figures scrawled in a red accounts book. 'Makes good packing material, shredded paper. Biodegradable. Better than your polystyrene stuff.'

Arthur had a brief vision of himself trying to paste together strips of shredded newspaper like an impossibly complicated jigsaw. Even assuming he could find the shreds. 'Well, thanks,' he said, sighed, and turned to go.

'No problem,' the newsagent called without looking up from his figures. 'You'll come back, won't you – if you ever want to *buy* anything.'

He had the newspaper on the desk by the computer in the little spare bedroom. Arthur had already looked for a table of contents or an index that might tell him what article or news item had been cut out. But newspapers didn't work like that. However, he had found a large box which listed phone numbers and addresses. The newspaper offices must keep back-issues, he reasoned, even if newsagents didn't. But the offices were the other side of the river and they would be closing soon, if they hadn't already.

The woman who eventually answered the phone sounded hassled. There was a pause when Arthur explained what he was after. A pause followed by a sigh.

'It's for a school project,' Arthur hazarded.

But this did not help. 'Young man,' the woman said, in a tone that conjured up an image of a severe, pencil-thin woman with her hair in a bun and a nose like a beak. 'Young man, if you think we have time to go rummaging through our old papers and reading them out over the telephone, then you are very sadly mistaken.'

'It's just one short article,' Arthur protested. 'It's important.'

But she did not seem to be listening. 'May I suggest that, if you wish to know what is in our newspaper, you go out and buy a copy.'

'I tried,' Arthur insisted. 'But it was last week's…'

The dial tone was loud in his ear, so he gave up. After he put down the phone he could still hear a humming and he realised the computer was on. The screen had been turned off, but the system was running.

What was the news article on page 9 of last week's *Cannon Street Bugle*, just above the headline 'Local Traders up in Arms'?

Arthur had looked at the website for the paper, but it was just a list of phone numbers and a box to send comments. He had considered asking about the article, but decided that he would get no more help than he had by phone. So instead he asked the *Invisible-Detective.com* website.

He had used the website before – you typed in a question and the answer was then e-mailed to you. It was supposed to be constructed by a computer which scoured the Internet for answers. But some of the e-mails Arthur had received were rather odd, to say the least. He had spent a while wondering who ran the site and how they knew the answers to some of the specific questions he had asked, based on what he had read in the Invisible Detective's casebook. They could not know that he had the book, or even who he was – his e-mail address was a random collection of numbers and letters that had been pre-installed on the computer when they bought it.

Arthur left the computer connected to the Internet while he went and got a drink of milk. There probably wouldn't be a reply until tomorrow, and it probably wouldn't be helpful. But he heard the mail arriving 'ping' as he walked back up the stairs. He ran to open his e-mail, sloshing milk on to the desk in his hurry. He wiped the mess away with the side of his hand, then licked it. It tasted of milk and polish.

The message read:

You already know where to look for the answers, Arthur.

He stared at it, read it again. And even as he wondered how whoever or whatever had written the reply knew his name, he realised that the answer to his problem was indeed obvious. It was Wednesday. On Wednesday the local library was open until eight o'clock. And the local library kept back-issues of the paper.

It was nearly always the same woman working in the library on a Wednesday evening. She was tall and thin with grey hair. Her glasses hung on a chain round her neck and she perched them precariously on the end of her nose so that she could look down it and through them at Arthur. When she saw who it was, she smiled.

'Oh, it's you.'

This was a first. Arthur did not think he had ever seen her smile before and he wondered what bad news she was about to give him that had so amused her.

'I was wondering if I could look at the local papers again,' Arthur said politely. He had his hands clasped behind his back and hoped he looked respectable enough for her.

'Of course. You know where the microfilms are and how to work the reader now, don't you?'

For a moment he was stunned. What had happened to the usual interrogation – the What do you want that for? Why? How long will you be? Are you sure that is the best use of your time? Have you considered all the other resources we have available?

'Er…' he said. 'Er…'

She was still smiling. It was not much of a smile, more of a pursing and twitching of her thin lips, but it seemed intended to be friendly. Encouraged, Arthur went on, 'It's only last week's, actually. I thought you'd probably have a copy.'

The smile faded. 'Last week's paper,' she said, in a tone that suggested this was not real research at all and that Arthur was somehow insulting the library by using it for so mundane a matter. 'You will find it in the rack next to the table where we keep *this* week's papers. We keep them for a month before we file them.' She removed her glasses and let them fall on their chain and bounce against her chest. 'Some people like to do last week's

92

crossword and then check their answers straight away,' she said with evident disapproval. 'Which makes it far too easy to cheat, in my opinion.'

'Oh, no,' Arthur said quickly. 'I just want to read an article I missed.'

The lady librarian raised an eyebrow and nodded. Taking this for as much of an indication of approval and permission as he was likely to get, Arthur mumbled a thank-you and went to find the rack of papers. As he crossed the library, someone got up from one of the reading tables as he approached. He glanced across at the movement and saw to his surprise that it was Sarah Bustle.

'I thought you'd be here,' she said, as he drew level. She tilted her head to one side so that her long dark hair hung down in a mass over one shoulder. Her mouth twitched into what was almost a smile. Then, without waiting for Arthur to answer, she strode swiftly away.

Arthur recognised the headlines on the front of the paper from Grandad's copy and took it to the reading table. Hurriedly, he turned to page nine, half expecting to find someone had mysteriously snipped out the same article in this copy of the paper as well.

But they had not. There it was, immediately above the local traders complaining about the plans for a new supermarket.

The Monster Returns?

The discovery of another mutilated cat close to where several others were found last week has led to rumours that a monster may be loose in London. Of course, there are no reported sightings, and a spokeswoman for the Metropolitan Police dismissed the suggestion as 'fanciful nonsense'. Henry Gladville, a local vet, confirmed that the cat had suffered multiple injuries and lacerations but gave his opinion that this was the work of a large predator such as a fox or a dog.

Arthur skimmed through a section where the cat's owners (and their nine-year-old daughter) were interviewed and expressed their distress and sadness in a series of short quotes.

Rumours of a monster seem to stem from

before the Second World War when local residents recall that a number of cats were found mutilated in the area. But then, as now, the existence of a cat-killing monster roaming the streets was denied by the local police.

There was more, but it added little. Arthur sat back and stared into space. Rumours that a monster was killing cats in the neighbourhood hardly seemed reason enough for an old man to disappear from his residential home. Except that Arthur had read the Invisible Detective's casebook. And, like his grandfather, he knew that the monster of the 1930s was more than just a fanciful rumour.

Chapter 6

They were not where they had said they would be. But Art was not worried by that. The night had turned decidedly chilly, so he expected Jonny and Flinch were sheltering behind the wall. When he found they were not there, he decided they might be in the yard behind Mr Fredericks's house.

But the yard was empty. The door to the toilet hut was open, swinging slightly in the night breeze. Otherwise all was still and silent. They were expecting him at eleven and it was a few minutes before, so perhaps they had gone for a walk to keep warm.

As he turned to go back to the broken wall and wait for them there, Art noticed that the kitchen door was also open. Jonny and Flinch might have gone inside. Maybe, he thought as he crossed the yard, they had seen or heard something. After all, it was always possible that there really *was* a monster. Or something.

The house was dark and silent apart from the distant sound of snoring. Art did not like to call out in case he woke Mr Fredericks. The moonlight spilled in through the small windows and the open door, puddling on the floor. As his eyes adjusted, Art could see that the kitchen was a mess. There were bits of broken crockery strewn across the floor, and the carpet was worn through and tattered as if someone had pulled at the threads and scratched at the fabric. Even in the semi-darkness, it reminded Art of the rolls of rotting carpet back at the den.

The den. It occurred to Art that if Flinch had got too tired she would have wanted to go home to the den. Jonny would have insisted on going with her rather than let her walk back alone through the dark streets. It was not far, and Jonny could run fast enough to be back to meet Art at eleven.

Except that it was eleven now, and Jonny was nowhere to be seen. The kitchen was a mess, but that meant nothing. Mr Fredericks had dropped a plate. Art had not noticed before how worn the carpet was. Or, he realised, how black and stained and grubby the sink was. Or the mud across the damp floor…

Maybe Jonny had gone for a take-away. Art frowned at the sudden thought. A take-away what? He would try the den, he decided. Probably he would meet Jonny on his way back to the house, all apologies for neglecting his duties. Over-anxious as always.

He did not meet Jonny on the way, and Art was pretty sure he had not passed him. In the diffident glow of the streetlamps, the warehouse they had made their den looked grim and foreboding. The broken windows were sightless eyes that watched Art make his way down the side alley and in through a small door. Inside, the stacked rolls of carpet seemed like blunted mountains on either side of him as he went through to the main area. Flinch usually slept in the corner of the big room, huddled into a pile of fabric they had spent a whole afternoon beating free of dust. Art could remember them choking and wheezing in the thick air. It had taken days to settle.

But there was no sign of Flinch. No sign of Jonny either. Art stood in the corner of the room and, despite his rising nerves, he yelled their names at the top of his voice. His only reply was a flurry of wings outside one of the high windows, where he had disturbed a bat or an owl, and the distant rumble of a passing car.

By now Art was feeling lonely and anxious.

He considered going to Jonny's house. But it was late and he did not want to get Jonny into trouble if he had slipped away. Art was sure Jonny would not have gone home without waiting for him. At the very least he would have left a message at the warehouse. And in any case, where was Flinch? The more he thought through the possibilities, the more worried Art became.

He closed the warehouse door quietly behind him. Dad was working tonight, though Art did not like the idea of enlisting his help to find his lost friends, who shouldn't have been out anyway. His dad thought he was himself tucked up at home in bed.

There was only one explanation, Art decided. And the more he thought about it, the more obvious it seemed. Mr Fredericks had seen Jonny and Flinch keeping watch – or perhaps they had gone to the house for some reason. He had invited them in out of the cold and, while he was snoring upstairs, Jonny and Flinch had fallen asleep in the sitting room. Maybe they just had not realised the time and were even now out by the broken wall wondering what had happened to Art.

He would not tell them how worried he had

been, Art decided. Better to say he had been delayed, that he was sorry he was late. He sprinted across the waste ground at the back of the house, almost turning his ankle at one point. There was still no sign of Jonny and Flinch – typical, they had to be asleep in the house. Again he let himself quietly into the kitchen and walked quickly to the sitting-room door, careful to avoid the broken china. The floor was damp under his feet and he could feel what was left of the carpet give slightly.

There were the remains of a fire in the grate. The embers glowed softly and reassuringly in the gloom. He could see a huddled shape in an armchair which he could tell at once was Flinch curled up into a ball.

Except that when he reached out to touch it gently, it was just a cushion and a blanket.

The stairs led down directly into the side of the sitting-room. As he stood in the darkness, wondering what to do next, Art heard one of the boards creak. With a deep breath of relief, he turned to see if it was Flinch or Jonny – he was certain it would be one of them.

But it was Mr Fredericks. The man was dressed, though his shirt was untucked and his eyes were wide with surprise and the remains of shaken-off sleep in the meagre light from the fire. His voice was husky and dry: 'What are you doing here?'

Startled, Art stammered, 'I – I... I was looking for my friends. I thought they were here.'

'Here?' Mr Fredericks was in the room now. 'Why would they be here?'

'We were worried about you,' Art confessed. 'They were keeping watch. For the monster,' he added. It sounded unconvincing and lame.

But Mr Fredericks did not seem to be angry to find Art in his house, merely confused. 'I saw them,' he said quietly. He sank down into the chair on top of what Art had thought was Flinch. 'Or did I dream it?'

'Saw them? Outside?'

'It must have been a dream. I heard something, went to the window to look.'

'And you saw them?' Art could hear the urgency in his own voice.

Mr Fredericks nodded. 'But it was a dream,' he insisted. 'I saw them jumping down into the storm drain.'

Art just stared at him.

'Why would they do that?' Mr Fredericks wondered, shaking his head. 'I must get back to bed. You'll let yourself out?'

'Yes,' Art said quietly. 'A dream.' He walked through to the kitchen in a daze. He closed the door carefully behind him, but it had warped or bent and did not shut properly. He caught sight of the distinctive dark shape of a rat as it ran across the yard, avoiding the dappled moonlight.

'I'll get Meg,' Art said out loud.

'What?' Meg's distinctive auburn curls emerged from a window next to the one that Art had been throwing small stones at.

'I need to talk to you,' he hissed, looking round furtively.

'Then don't throw stones at *Mum's* window,' she hissed back. 'She needs her sleep, and I doubt you want to talk to *her* at gone midnight any more than she wants to talk to you.'

It was only just after midnight, but Art didn't press the point. In any case, Meg's head was disappearing back inside and the window swung shut. He waited under the streetlamp and, after what seemed an age, the front door opened and

Meg came out.

She was wrapped in a large coat, which flapped open as she hurried over to him, revealing she was fully dressed.

'You took a long time,' Art said.

'Dad's asleep on the sofa. Goodness knows when he got in. I had to tiptoe past. Couldn't you have waited till six o'clock, when I came to keep watch?' she demanded.

Art took a deep breath. 'I'm probably being daft,' he said, 'but Flinch and Jonny have disappeared.'

'What do you mean?' They were hurrying along the pavement now, in the direction of Cannon Street.

'I went to take over from Jonny and they weren't there. Either of them.'

'Maybe they got bored. Or cold.' Meg pulled her coat tighter round her to make the point.

'But they're not back at the den. And they didn't go inside the house. I spoke to Mr Fredericks,' he admitted. 'He said he dreamed he saw them jump into that storm drain.'

Meg gave a 'harumph'. 'Not very likely.'

'I know. But,' Art admitted, 'I'm worried.'

'Yes,' Meg said quietly. 'Mr Fredericks may have seen something. Maybe I'll be able to tell if I talk to him. Let's try to talk to him again. At least we can check if Flinch and Jonny have turned up yet.'

'Good idea.'

Meg was walking quicker now, striding in front of Art. 'You should have got me sooner,' she said.

They let themselves in through the twisted kitchen door. Art called for Mr Fredericks from the bottom of the stairs – cautiously at first, embarrassed to be back yet again, disturbing the poor man's sleep. There was no answer, so he tried again louder.

After several minutes of getting no response, he went carefully up the stairs. He could not hear the sound of snoring this time. Meg stood, arms folded, in the sitting-room, watching him.

There were two tiny bedrooms upstairs. One was obviously not used. It smelled musty and several chairs were stacked up in a corner. The other room was almost filled with a bed. The covers were pulled back and the curtains were open.

But the room was empty. Mr Fredericks had vanished.

Art stared at the empty bed. Through the window he could see out across the waste ground towards the River Thames in the distance. A moon was shining on the murky rippling waters like a nervous twin of the real one in the sky above. Wondering what to do now, Art turned and stepped back on to the tiny landing at the top of the stairs – little more than an enlarged top step. 'He isn't here,' he called down the stairs. 'Mr Fredericks has vanished too.'

'There's someone coming,' Meg called back softly from the room below.

Art could already hear the sound of heavy, booted feet in the yard outside the front of the house. A moment later someone started hammering on the front door.

'What do we do?' Meg asked as Art hastened down the stairs.

'We open the door.'

Outside several tall, broad figures stood waiting, silhouetted against the dark grey sky. One of them stepped forwards and

Art stumbled back in surprise. Behind him, Meg gave a gasp of astonishment.

'Well, well, well,' the man said slowly in a deep voice. 'I don't know exactly what I expected to find here. But it certainly wasn't you, Arthur Drake.'

Before long the house was alive with light. There was no electricity, but the policemen found oil lamps and candles. Meg and Art stood awkwardly in the front room while Art's father walked all round them, as if still unable to believe his eyes.

'It's a long story, Dad,' Art said.

'I bet it is.' He stopped in front of Meg. 'Do your parents know where you are?'

'Not exactly.'

'We were keeping watch,' Art explained. 'At least, Jonny and Flinch were. But they've disappeared.'

'Gone home to bed, I expect. And why, may I ask, are you keeping watch in a murdered man's home?'

'Murdered?' Art and Meg stared at each other.

'You mean Mr Fredericks?' Meg asked. Her

face was pale in the flickering light.

Art's dad nodded. 'We've only just managed to identify him. The body was found last week. Stabbed.'

'Last week?' Art could not believe this. 'You're sure it was Mr Fredericks.'

'We are now. Why?'

'Part of the long story,' Meg said, before Art could answer.

Art's dad inspected them both for a few moments more. 'I'll talk to you after school tomorrow,' he said to Art at last. 'When we both have the time for long stories. Or tall ones, as the case may be. Now, off home, the pair of you. And don't dilly-dally on the way.'

They went out the back through the kitchen without a word. Art picked up an oil lamp from beside the sink as he passed, and saw Meg glance at him. She knew what he was intending.

Only when they were out in the yard, the door pushed as closed as it would go behind them, did Meg speak. 'It wasn't the cat at all.'

'What do you mean?'

'That explains everything, don't you see?'

'No,' Art confessed, 'I don't.'

She sighed. 'Mr Fredericks was so upset, so shocked. More than you'd expect if he'd just lost his cat. '

'I suppose.'

'But he hadn't, had he? That's the point.' She sighed again, annoyed that Art hadn't reached the same conclusions she had. 'It was his *brother* he was grieving for. The same surname, the same address. That's who it must be.'

'And you think he sort of transferred his shock and grief to the cat?'

They were standing beside the dark hole of the storm drain now. 'He's too shocked even to admit his brother's gone,' Meg said. 'I knew he wasn't telling us the whole truth. He wouldn't even tell it to himself.'

'Yes,' Art said. 'I suppose you're right.' He handed her the oil lamp and looked down into the murky depths of the drain. 'Here, hold this a minute while I climb down.'

'Wilkins,' Sergeant Drake shouted.

The constable appeared in the doorway to the main room. 'Sir?'

'Go after those two kids, will you? Make sure

they get home all right.'

'I'm sure they know the way –' Wilkins started.

But Drake cut him off. 'Just do it, will you, Constable? It's nearly one o'clock in the morning and I don't want them wandering about London on their own.'

Wilkins sighed and nodded. 'Yes, sir. I'll see if I can catch up with them.'

The moon was full and bright as Wilkins crossed the yard at the back of the house. He had decided he would cross the waste ground and, if he could not see the two youngsters by the time he reached the other side, he would return to the house.

In fact, he saw them almost at once – disappearing down a hole in the ground. He hesitated for a moment, wondering whether to tell Drake or simply to go after them and find out what they were playing at. He ought to tell Drake, he knew. But if he didn't follow them straight away, he might never find them again. 'Children!' he muttered angrily as he made his decision.

The light from the lamp was not the only

illumination. Weak moonlight shone hesitantly through drains and cracks in the crumbling roof of the tunnel. For a while the tunnel sloped downwards, then it levelled off. It was just high enough for Meg to stand, though Art had to bend slightly to avoid banging his head on the uneven roof.

'Oh, what are we doing?' Meg wanted to know. They were standing in over a foot of water. Water that was cold and smelly and coated with scum and dirt.

'Just checking.' Art held the lamp up so that it cast its light further along the crumbling brick of the circular tunnel. 'Mr Fredericks says he dreamed that Jonny and Flinch came down here.'

'And how do you know it wasn't just that – a dream?' She had her arms folded and her head cocked to one side. Art could tell she was annoyed.

'Because of this.' He sloshed through the water to the side wall a little ahead of them. There was a damp patch on the wall where mildew and fungus were growing, covering a large area of the brickwork. Someone had scraped away at the dark growth to reveal the pale masonry below. Art traced the lines with his finger, feeling the brick crack and powder under the slight pressure.

Meg could see it as well – two letters scraped on to the wall. J and F. 'Jonny and Flinch,' she said out loud.

'Seems likely.'

'But why? Why did they come down here?'

'I don't know. But I think we should find them.' Art lowered the lamp slightly and they could see now that there was an arrow scratched under the letters – an arrow pointing deeper and further into the tunnel. 'This way, it seems.'

It was slow progress, forcing their feet through the thick water. After what seemed like an age, they reached a point where the tunnel split in two.

'Which way now?' Meg asked. 'Or should we each try a different tunnel?'

'I don't think that's a good idea. If the tunnels split more – and I think they will – then we could end up getting lost down here.'

'What, then?'

Art was peering down one of the tunnels. 'What's that?' Just at the limit of the lamplight he could see something floating on the water, something pale, a rectangle of white in the gloom.

They made their way down towards it and before long they could see that it was a piece of paper. Meg plucked it from the water and held it dripping in front of the lamp. It was a five-pound note.

'We're rich,' she said with a laugh. Five pounds was a huge amount of money.

'Richer than you think,' Art said slowly. 'Look.' He pointed down the tunnel. Again, just at the limit of the lamplight, they could both see another pale rectangle of paper undulating with the water.

'Ten pounds?' Meg said in an awed whisper. She was already wading towards it. 'Art!' Her voice was strained with excitement and emotion as she picked up the second banknote.

'What?'

'There's another one.'

As soon as he reached her, Art held the lamp up to the ceiling so that the light shone as far ahead of them as possible. A drain further along the tunnel afforded more pale light. And in that light Art could see a line of white patches on the water. He counted another four, stretching out along the tunnel in a trail.

'Jonny and Flinch must have left them,' Art said. 'Five-pound notes…'

'But where did they get them?' Meg asked. She leaned against the side of the tunnel as she examined the two wet notes she was holding. But the wall crumbled away behind her, unable to take the weight. She screamed, dropping the notes and flailing her arms to try to regain her balance. Art grabbed one of her arms and pulled her upright again.

'This place is falling apart,' he said. 'Are you all right?'

Meg nodded, biting her lip. 'I think so. But what about Jonny and Flinch – what's happened to them?'

'Let's follow the money and find out.'

From somewhere in the distance came a sound. It echoed and rang round the tunnel, making them both pause. It was impossible to tell whether it came from in front or behind. It sounded like a voice, except it was distorted, reverberating. Inhuman. But while it was indistinct, the words it was shouting were clear enough.

'Arthur Drake…' the unearthly voice called. 'Arthur Drake…'

There was only one place left that Arthur could think of going. It was almost nine o'clock and it was already dark, but the antiques shop was on the way home. And in any case, his dad was working that night so he would not know how late Arthur got back.

The shop would be closed, of course. But it was at the shop that Arthur had first learned of the Invisible Detective. It was at the shop that he had been given the casebook and the strange pebble that he could stare into and see the past… It had to be worth looking at least.

There was a light on. The sign said 'Closed' but Arthur could see the glow of light from the back room even through the thick dust that covered the glass panel in the door. He cupped his hands to the glass and pressed his face into them to try to see better without reflections from the cars and neon in the street behind him. The city was quiet so late in the evening. Even some of the pubs closed early, once the traders and bankers had gone home and business was slow.

Slowly his eyes grew accustomed to the faint light inside the shop and he could make out shapes in the gloom. There was a chess set laid out on a table in mid-game. A battered leather armchair. Cabinets and display cases ranged across the room, punctuated by stacks of books and papers, obscured by dust and bric-à-brac and still more dust. And then, suddenly, eyes staring back at him through the glass.

Arthur gave a yelp of surprise and leaped back. A moment later, the door swung open and the wizened old shopkeeper stepped out on to the pavement.

'Come in, come in,' he said in his cracked, dusty voice, motioning for Arthur to follow him back into the shop.

'I'm sorry,' Arthur told him as he stepped inside. 'I was just looking.'

'Just looking?' The man seemed amused. He led Arthur through the clutter and towards the back of the shop, towards the door where the light was shining.

'Well,' Arthur admitted, 'I wanted to ask you something.'

'Oh? About the Invisible Detective, perhaps?'

'Sort of. About the monster that they hunted for back then. About...' He stopped and tried to decide what he really did want to ask. He wanted to know what had happened to Grandad, but to work that out he needed to know about the monster. 'Just, well – what's going on?'

'You mean, with the monster?'

'Do you know?'

The man paused in the doorway and turned to face Arthur. 'I only know,' he said slowly, 'what your grandfather has told me.'

Arthur caught his breath. 'And what's that?'

The old man was smiling now. He stepped aside to allow someone else to emerge from the back room of the shop. 'Why not ask him yourself?'

'I knew you'd come here sooner or later,' Arthur's grandad said. He was smiling, obviously pleased he had been right. 'I need your help, young man,' he said. 'To find the monster.'

Chapter 7

'Arthur Drake!' There was still no answer, so Constable Wilkins gave up shouting along the tunnel. He could hear his voice echoing back to him. It sounded distorted and strangely inhuman. He glanced round at the moonlight falling through the entrance, then sighed, raised the lantern he was carrying and started down the tunnel.

'What was it?' Flinch asked, her voice strained and tired.

'I don't know,' Jonny told her. 'Sounded like someone shouting. Maybe it's Art.'

'Do you think he'll find us?'

'Of course he will.' Jonny turned away. Even in the dim light she might see how uncertain and worried he looked. 'He'll follow the trail.'

After they had run down the tunnel to escape the rats that leaped after them, Jonny and Flinch had quickly become lost. Jonny had a torch but its battery was almost exhausted and so they were in near-darkness. He had managed to scrape a crude 'J' and 'F' on a patch of mossy wall with the back of the torch before they ran from the rats and hoped someone would see the letters.

They had tried to retrace their steps, but whichever way they turned they found only more tunnels. Occasionally there was a drain set into the roof and they could see the moon struggling through. But shouting attracted no attention, and, even if they could have reached up and moved the drain covers aside, the openings were too small for even Flinch to squeeze through.

They had been down in the damp, smelly, crumbling tunnels for what seemed like hours when Flinch spotted something. She was carrying the torch as its weakening beam picked out a pale area on the dark wall ahead of them. When they reached it, wading through water that was almost up to Flinch's waist, they discovered it was a collection of wood, paper and a blanket. The wood looked as if it had been torn from crates and packing cases, and the blanket was draped over the top. But most of the area was filled with what looked like stacks of paper. When Flinch lifted the blanket, they could see that it was resting on more piles of paper.

From the way some of the stacks of paper

were leaning haphazardly, it looked as if whoever had left them there had been in a hurry. There was enough light from the torch for Jonny to make out that some of the papers had fallen free and were floating in the water. Flinch picked one up and gave a gasp of astonishment.

They were not just pieces of paper. They were banknotes – thousands of five-pound notes just dumped in the sewer.

'We're rich,' Jonny exclaimed.

'Don't be daft,' Flinch told him. 'It's not ours.'

'It's not anybody's, not down here.'

'Course it someone's. They'll come back for it.' She carefully placed the notes she had retrieved from the water on top of the pile and smoothed them down. 'I hope they come soon,' she said.

'I don't.' Jonny was looking round anxiously, in case whoever had left the money was already making their way along the tunnels towards them.

'Why not?'

'Look,' he said impatiently, 'where do you think this money came from? It isn't just kept here by someone who pops down now and again to refill his wallet and pay the bills.'

Flinch frowned. 'Money's kept in a bank,' she said, and her face cleared. 'The robbery?'

'That's right. Art said they tunnelled in through the sewers, remember? And I'm not sure I want to meet whoever it was that left it here.' He picked up a stack of notes and riffled through them. 'You're right, it's not our money. But unless we can get out of here and tell someone, whoever robbed the bank will get away with it.' He replaced the money and put his hand on Flinch's shoulder, sorry that he had snapped at her earlier. 'I'm worried that we've been going round in circles. We need some way of marking where we've been.'

'Like the arrow we left for Art and Meg?'

Jonny nodded. 'It was lucky there was that patch of mould. We won't be able to mark these walls so easily. But I want to leave some sort of sign so we can see and know we've already been this way.'

Flinch was staring at the money again. 'If we don't get out, the robbers will keep the money.'

'Yes.'

She lifted down as much of the money as she

could easily hold – a thick stack of notes. 'Then let's leave a trail. We'll float these on the water to show where we've been.'

'That's not a bad idea,' Jonny agreed. 'There's no current. So unless it rains or something, the notes should stay pretty much where we leave them. Let's do it.'

He gave Flinch a quick, gentle hug and was rewarded with a wide grin.

But a long time later, they had run out of five-pound notes, and their attempts to retrace their steps to the stack of money and start hunting again for a way out were thwarted when they came to an intersection of tunnels where there seemed to be no notes floating on the water any more.

'We need to get some rest and try again,' Jonny decided. He could see that Flinch was exhausted and almost in tears. They had both been up all night.

There was a narrow shelf running at his shoulder height along the edge of one of the intersecting tunnels. He helped Flinch up, then heaved himself after her. They lay there dripping, and Jonny took the torch from Flinch and switched it off. They huddled together in the near-darkness. Before long, Jonny could hear Flinch's breathing become rhythmic and relaxed as she slipped into sleep. Despite being so tired, he was sure he would never be able to sleep.

So it was a shock and a surprise to find himself jolted awake by the sound of distant shouting.

'You can't tell which way it's coming from,' Flinch said, already wide awake.

'But at least it means someone's down here, looking for us probably.'

'It might be the robbers,' Flinch warned.

'I doubt they'd be shouting. They'd want to keep quiet.'

'Unless they're lost too,' Flinch said. 'Or they're annoyed someone's taken some of the money.'

Jonny was lowering himself off the ledge and into the shallow water as she said this, preparing to shout back and call for help. He paused. That was a point. Maybe attracting attention was not such a good idea, not until they knew who was down in the sewers with them.

* * *

Constable Wilkins was coming to the realisation that unless he made his way back to the tunnel entrance, he would soon be lost. He had kept count of the left and right turns he had made along the tunnels, but much further and they would begin to blur in his mind. Added to this, it was uncomfortable to walk stooped along the tunnels, pushing his way through the water. For a while he had taken his helmet off, but after bumping his head several times on jutting bricks in the low roof, he put it back on and bent further to compensate.

One more junction, he decided. Just one more. Then he must head back and confess to Sergeant Drake that he had not managed to find the children. There was always a chance, of course, that they had got round behind him and were no longer down in the tunnels. Certainly they were not answering his shouts. All he could hear was his own voice echoing back to him by a different route.

As he made his way along the tunnel, Wilkins happened to glance into the dark opening of a side tunnel. It was not one he had explored and he found he could see a light shining further along.

Dawn was creeping around the heavy iron bars of a storm drain, shining into a corner where the tunnel bent sharply away. The corner was raised above the main tunnel, like a shelf, so that it was clear of the muck and water of the tunnel floor. By his reckoning Wilkins decided the drain could not be far from where he had entered the tunnel system. Possibly it was somewhere else on the same area of waste ground.

But as he approached, it was not the light shining through the drain in the roof that held Wilkins's attention. It was what the light was falling on.

At first it looked like a pile of wood and other debris washed down the drains and deposited on the raised shelf. The broken side of a packing case, the shattered carcass of a tea chest, even the remains of a threadbare blanket – and not just washed haphazardly into the crook of the tunnel. They had been carefully arranged, the wood round the edge and the blanket crumpled into the middle. It looked, bizarrely, like a bed.

Now that he was standing right next to it, his lantern raised, Wilkins could see over the top of the debris. There were other things on the shelf behind the 'bed'. He reached out in surprise, his hand closing on a battered bank deposit box. It had been broken open, but as he lifted it a heavy necklace fell into Wilkins's hand. He could see other boxes scattered back into the recess. A bundle of banknotes was pushed back into the furthest corner, and he could see now that he was so close that the blanket was resting on a bed of banknotes, as if to form a cushion for whoever slept there.

He ran his hand round the inside of the blanket. It formed a large area. A bed, perhaps, for someone almost as big as himself. And as he removed his hand, Wilkins realised that despite the dampness of the air and the cold chill of early morning, the blanket was warm. As if whoever slept there had only just got out of their bed.

Best to get back to the entrance and go for help, Wilkins decided. But even as he turned, he could hear someone sloshing through the shallow water behind him. Someone or something. A dark shadow seemed to detach itself from the tunnel wall and Wilkins gave a startled cry. His hand convulsed in surprise and the lantern slipped from his grasp. It splashed with a hiss into the water at his feet. The only light now was behind him, shining through the drain above.

The black shape seemed almost to rear up, a skeletal shadow that reached out for him. He backed away in fright, but his back met the slick wetness of the tunnel wall below the ledge. One foot skidded on the slippery floor and he had to scrabble at the ledge to save himself from falling. It was an instinctive reaction.

If he *had* fallen, Wilkins realised, he might have slipped beneath the claw-like hands that whipped out towards his neck. But it was too late now. Too late to duck, too late to run, too late to try to push the black shape away... Too late for anything but a high-pitched, broken scream of terror.

'That came from down there,' Meg said.

Art had heard it too – a choked-off scream that echoed along the tunnel system. They stood stock still in the ensuing silence.

'Are you sure?' Art whispered at last. He could not say which direction the actual sound had come from, it was lost in its own echoes.

'Oh, come on,' she insisted, grabbing Art's hand and pulling him along.

Soon they came to a side tunnel and paused. Looking along the tunnel, Art could see the early-morning light shining through a drain and illuminating a shelf in the corner as the tunnel bent sharply away. There seemed to be something on the ledge. It looked like a body, its legs bent and one arm extended along the ledge.

Hesitantly, they edged along the tunnel, both watching for any sign of movement. They were almost at the body before Art realised his mistake and laughed nervously. What he had thought was a body was nothing of the sort.

'It's like a bed,' Meg said.

What had been an arm was now a loop of faded, torn blanket. The bent legs were actually the remains of a packing case. He could see dark shapes beyond the falling light. It looked like a pile of banknotes shoved into the corner, and he put the oil lamp down carefully beside the blanket.

'I thought it was a body,' Art said, relieved.

Meg tapped his shoulder. 'I think you might be right,' she said. Her voice was husky and breathless and she was pointing at something in the murky water beside them on the tunnel floor.

Art stared down where she was pointing.

There was something dark half-submerged in the water. As he watched, a pale hand bobbed to the surface to float beside what Art could now see was a policeman's helmet. He reached out tentatively towards it, meaning to turn the body over, though he was sure the man was dead. He was face down, not moving except with the movement of the water. Meg caught his hand as he reached out, and Art looked up to see what she was looking at on the other side of the tunnel.

For the briefest moment the tunnel was gone. He had an impression of rough concrete in place of the decaying bricks, a dry cement floor, cables and wires running along the wall and punctuated by metal tags and warning notices.

But almost immediately the image disappeared. It was just the crumbling darkness of the tunnel. And in the darkness an even darker shape was detaching itself from the gloom, rearing up in front of them like a huge, hungry animal.

'It can't be the same monster,' Arthur said. 'Can it?'

Grandad shook his head. He was breathing heavily from the long walk and talking was an obvious effort. 'Another one,' he wheezed. 'I think they sent it to find the first one. It must have... slept. Or something.'

'Perhaps they hibernate,' Arthur suggested.

The courtyard off St Swithin's Lane where Mr Fredericks's house had been was long gone. A huge monster of concrete and glass rose up in its place, lights still blazing on some of the upper floors. The name and logo of a City bank was stencilled on to the glass of the doors and in the foyer a security guard yawned behind an enormous expanse of wood and chrome.

'You really think its still down there?'

They walked past the impressive doors and kept going slowly along the lane. After a few yards, Grandad paused and bent to get his breath back. 'Don't know,' he said. 'But have to be sure.' He looked up at Arthur through watery eyes. 'You read the newspaper report?'

Arthur nodded. 'Yes, but – I mean... a few dead cats.'

'I know, I know.' The old man was breathing

more easily now. 'But that's how it started last time. And there have been other stories, other news reports over the past year.' He set off again, slowly, along the lane. 'It lives down there. Perhaps it just forages for food when it gets hungry and can't find anything in the tunnels.'

'So why is that a problem?' Arthur was feeling cold inside – nervous, anxious, worried. 'Or if it is, why can't we just tell the police – tell Dad?'

Grandad smiled in the light from a window. 'Just tell Dad,' he mused. 'How many times did I wonder about that, eh?' He gave a short laugh and kept walking. 'We have to be sure. We need something to say, before we can tell.'

'So where are we going?'

'There are other ways into the tunnel system,' Grandad said. 'Don't you remember?'

'Sort of.' It was strange. Arthur could read the words in the casebook – he had read them all, so many times. But it was as if they failed to stick in his mind. Like a dream that slipped away with the morning light. Then, later, it would come back like a memory that had slept and been recalled by some event or sound or word or smell... 'It's as if I can only remember what happened when the time is right,' he said. He had not thought of it in that way before, but somehow he was sure that was what it was.

'Hmm,' Grandad said.

They had reached the end of the lane and he turned to the right. He was breathing heavily again with the exertion, but he did not seem about to slow down.

'That business with the puppets,' Arthur went on, hurrying to keep up. 'I read about it in the casebook – in *your* casebook. But it was only when I checked things in the library and when I got those e-mails and stuff that I sort of *remembered* about it. What is it Dad says? "In one ear and out the other." It was like that with my brain.' He was talking for his own benefit as much as Grandad's. In fact, the old man seemed not to be listening. Perhaps he could not hear Arthur over his own desperate gasps for air.

He stopped at last, just as Arthur was beginning to think his grandfather might collapse before he slowed down. Drawing great rasping breaths, Grandad leaned forward with his hands on his knees. Still in this crouched pose, he swung round, looking for something on the ground.

'I'm sure it's here somewhere,' he murmured.

They were in a narrow street that Arthur was not sure he had seen before. It was just an ordinary street – offices down one side, a sandwich bar and a café on the corner. Opposite them was a grey mass that looked like a multi-storey car park.

'If only I had my casebook,' Grandad added. I remember drawing a map, afterwards. Showing where the sewer tunnels ran under the streets.'

Arthur grinned, despite his nervousness. He reached into his coat pocket and pulled out the battered leather-bound notebook. 'Will this do?'

Grandad's eyes widened. 'Good gracious,' he said quietly. 'You know I haven't seen that since Old Jerrickson…' His voice tailed off as he carefully opened the book. He seemed to have trouble turning the pages, though Arthur could not tell if it was because they were old and brittle, because his eyes seemed so moist or because his hands were refusing to cooperate.

Eventually he found the page he wanted. 'Here we are.' He angled the notebook so that Arthur could see. The pages were even more yellowed under the streetlamps' glare.

As soon as he saw it, Arthur remembered

that he had seen the map before. It was sketched in pencil, showing the streets and main buildings. Over that was drawn a thick, dark line showing where the tunnel system went. It looked a bit like the tube map, only less organised.

Grandad was tracing a crooked finger along the dark line. The finger paused, tapped gently, and Grandad looked up. 'Just along here, I think.'

He led Arthur a short way along the street, then crossed to the other side. 'Ah, yes. That will be it,' he said at last. He shuffled a few steps further along the pavement, as if suddenly exhausted by his previous athleticism.

'What?' Arthur hurried after him.

He was standing beside a rectangle of concrete set into the pavement. A manhole cover stamped with meaningless letters and edged with a metal strip. 'Yes. The nest was under here, I'm sure of it.'

'It was a drain,' Arthur said slowly. Now, suddenly, he could not only recall reading Art's description in the casebook, but also remember seeing it – if 'remember' was the right word. 'Iron bars across a hole at the side of the road.'

'It may have been moved slightly, but the tunnel is below us now.' Grandad was nodding to himself, convinced he was right.

'So now what?'

Grandad looked up, frowning as if he could not believe Arthur had to ask. 'We need to lift this cover off,' he said. 'And get down there.'

Grandad had a knife. It was a large, ornate dagger in a leather sheath that he produced from his inside jacket pocket and, with some difficulty, jammed down the side of the cover.

'Borrowed it from the shop,' he said. With shaking hands, he wriggled the blade further into the crack. Arthur did not need to ask what shop. 'Always come prepared.' He gave a last push on the carved wooden knife handle to check it would go in no further.

Arthur was not sure how this helped. 'Now what?'

'Now I pull the knife up, levering the cover. And you try to get a grip on the edge as it appears.'

The old man had to use both his hands, and Arthur could see the effort and pain of gripping the knife tightly. The cover came up just enough for Arthur to scrabble at it desperately with breaking fingernails. He managed to hold the heavy concrete and metal just long enough for Grandad to help him pull it a little further. The crack had widened as the cover came up and the knife slipped back in easily, levering again, getting under the cover. Arthur was able to get a better grip as more of the cover's edge was exposed, and there was enough play between the cover and the hole it was fitted into for them to manage to swing it up and over.

It clattered on to the pavement and Arthur looked round nervously in case anyone had heard or seen. But the street seemed empty. He glanced at his watch and saw to his astonishment that it was almost midnight. 'What am I doing?' he muttered, but he could see from Grandad's answering smile that he had heard.

The knife disappeared back into Grandad's jacket and he drew out a small torch.

'You were prepared, weren't you?' Arthur said. He was out of breath from the effort of lifting the cover.

Grandad was wheezing heavily again, pointing the torch waveringly into the dark hole at their feet. The juddering light picked out the dull rungs of a ladder set into the wall of the tunnel and played over a dry cement floor.

'Not a sewer any more,' Grandad rasped. 'Some sort of service tunnel maybe.'

'Are you up to this?' Arthur asked. He was worried Grandad might not be able to manage the ladder. Or worse, that once down he might never be able to climb back up.

The old man nodded. 'I'll be fine. You go first, I'll shine the torch for you.'

It was not a proper ladder at all, Arthur realised, as he lowered himself on to the first rung. It was just steel rods that had been bent and angled, then concreted into the wall. At least the tunnel was dry, not sloshing with dirty water, as it had been all those years ago, he thought.

Once he was at the bottom of the ladder, he reached up for the torch that Grandad was holding out to him. As he held it for his grandfather to follow precariously down, Arthur glanced along the tunnel. There was enough light from the torch and from the street above to make out the walls and to see a short way along. He did not like to look away for more than a couple of seconds at a time in case Grandad got into difficulty, but the old man seemed to be managing well.

The tunnel was not very large. Once out from under the raised section where the ladder went up, there would be barely enough height for Arthur to stand upright, and it was about four feet wide. The walls were smooth cement, and cables and wires were strung along them so they hung down in low loops. Every now and again Arthur could see glass covers set into the walls. He guessed they were lights, but he could see no way of switching them on. Probably there was a master switch at a control centre somewhere, or beneath a particular manhole cover.

Grandad finally made it to the floor and looked round cautiously. He was breathing heavily again and Arthur could see in the torchlight that his face was dripping with perspiration.

'I'm sorry, Arthur,' he gasped, 'but I think I'm about done in after all that.' He lowered himself carefully, using the lowest of the steel rungs as a support for his weight, until he was sitting on the floor.

'You OK?' Arthur stooped beside him and was answered with a thin smile.

'Just out of breath. Happens at my age.'

'You want to rest for a while before we look

137

round?' Arthur was not at all sure there was very much to see. Ten minutes in each direction, he hoped, would satisfy his grandad that there were no monsters any more, that the tunnels were cosy and safe and completely creature-free.

But Grandad was shaking his head. 'No, no. I'll wait here while you explore a bit.'

'On my own?' That sounded a little less enthusiastic than Arthur had intended. In fact, he thought, it sounded scared and whingy.

'I think we need to hurry, before anyone notices that cover is off. Besides,' he went on, 'one of us should stay here and make sure nobody puts it back. I don't think either of us could push it open, and there's not room for us both on the ladder.'

This was not making Arthur feel any less apprehensive. But he bit his lip and nodded. 'There's nothing down here,' he said.

'Then there's nothing to be frightened of. Don't go far. Stay within shouting distance, you know – just in case.'

'And what am I looking for? A monster?'

Grandad nodded, his face grave and serious in the torchlight. 'Or evidence of one. A nest, perhaps, like before. Signs of damage, habitation, food...'

'Monster droppings,' Arthur added. 'Great.' He forced himself to smile, angling the beam of the torch so that Grandad could see he wasn't frightened. 'I shan't be long. This way first, I think.'

'Complete waste of time,' Arthur muttered to himself as he walked slowly along the tunnel, his head tilted awkwardly and uncomfortably to one side to keep clear of the low roof. 'Monsters – yeah, right.'

The tunnel had taken a turn to the left, just out of sight of the ladder. It seemed, so far as Arthur could tell, to be following the course of the road above them. He was shining the torch along the walls, examining the cables and wires, and trying to interpret the letters and numbers attached to them on twisted metal tags. There was a sweet, sickly smell in the air, like old fruit.

'You all right?' he shouted back along the tunnel. He could almost taste that smell. His voice echoed round and he kept walking slowly onwards.

Arthur had taken several steps before he realised he had not heard a reply. At the same moment, his foot struck something on the floor in front of him. Something soft. 'Grandad?' he called again, stopping and shining the torch down at his feet.

His foot was up against a cat. A dead cat. It looked as if it had been dead for a long time. And as he moved the torch cautiously along the floor of the tunnel, Arthur could see that there were others – a pile of dead, rotting fur. Cats, rats, mice… Even a small dog. All piled up in the tunnel. As he stared in horrified disbelief, he realised he could taste the stench of them at the back of his mouth and he struggled not to retch.

'Grandad?' he called again, more hesitant now, voice wavering as the fear washed over him.

But again there was no reply. Arthur stood as still as he could, holding his breath as he listened, as he tried to keep the smell out of his nostrils. There was something, some sound. But it wasn't Grandad calling back to say he was all right and that he was being foolish and that it was just plain daft to think there might be a monster down in the tunnels with them.

It was a snuffling, scuffing, scratching sound that came from further down the tunnel – from beyond the heap of decaying animals… The torch beam lashed violently around the tunnel ceiling and walls as Arthur struggled to control his fear. The light spilled across the animals, showing where they had been torn apart, ripped open, eaten. And as Arthur managed to hold it steady, with both hands tightly gripping the torch, the light settled on the massive, dark shape that was scratching its monstrous way down the tunnel towards him.

Chapter 8

Art and Meg both clutched each other as they pressed back against the damp wall. In front of them, the dark shape shuffled forwards, sending water rippling across the tunnel to wash at their legs. Another lurching step and the shape was full in the dim light that shone in through the bars of the opening above them.

Meg gave a sigh of relief and pulled away from Art. He laughed, nervously, as the tension and fear fell away. 'Mr Fredericks!'

The old man looked a mess. His grey hair was slicked down over his forehead and he was drenched. It looked as if he had fallen into the shallow water several times, and possibly rolled around in it for good measure. There was a steady drip-drip of sound as he stood staring at them, wide-eyed.

'I – I – I – I thought it was the other two,' he stammered. 'I followed them, after you had gone. Not a dream, I realised. So I followed. But then… then…' He turned away, leaning against the tunnel wall for support. His weight shifted the bricks enough for a fine shower of powdered cement to sprinkle down from the roof and patter into the water.

'You got lost,' Meg finished for him. She made it sound like an accusation, and Mr Fredericks nodded, embarrassed. The oil lamp on the ledge behind her was throwing Meg's shadow, huge and distorted, across the tunnel wall opposite.

'But I did see the monster,' he said. The whites of his eyes seemed to glow in the tunnel. 'Back there somewhere. I saw the monster.' He sank down so that he was sitting in the water, but he seemed not to care.

Art stepped away from the man, gesturing for Meg to follow. 'He's scared out of his wits,' he whispered in her ear.

'His brother, remember,' she whispered back.

Art nodded. 'Best not to show him that dead policeman. Even mentioning a body might tip him over the edge. I don't know what's going on, but there's no monster down here.'

Mr Fredericks seemed to hear this, or perhaps he was merely noticing the blanket and banknotes for the first time. 'This is where it lives, do you see?' He pulled himself upright and leaned over the ledge to see the blanket and broken wood. 'It's made a nest.'

'Possibly,' Art conceded. 'But this looks more like a bed for a person than a nest for a monster.' The oil lamp was below the edge of the makeshift wooden frame, and the pale light from above cast shadows over the blanket. Now they could see that the indentation in the middle looked like a curled figure. Art traced it with his hand. 'Someone, not something, slept here, I think.'

'Whatever it is,' Meg said, 'we need to get help. Jonny and Flinch are down here somewhere, and maybe someone else too. If they think someone has found their loot...' She shrugged.

'Good point,' Art said. 'So let's find the trail of notes again and follow it back to the storm drain. We can get the police from the house.'

'Police?' Mr Fredericks's voice was a dry rasp of surprise.

'Yes,' Art told him, 'they came to the house. Your house.'

'Police,' he said again, his eyes unfocused.

Meg put her hand on his shoulder. 'It's all right,' she said. 'We know about your brother.'

Mr Fredericks said nothing. But his face was pale in the dim light.

The five-pound notes were getting saturated and some of them had sunk into the murky water.

'We'd better hurry or we'll lose the trail,' Meg said.

Mr Fredericks seemed to have recovered some of his composure. Perhaps the fact that they knew about his brother, Art thought, had jolted his mind closer to normality, helped him get over the shock. 'Shouldn't we collect up the money?' he asked.

'Best leave it,' Art decided. 'In case Jonny and Flinch need to follow.'

'If it hasn't sunk out of sight first,' Meg added.

They made slow progress, and at each intersection it was harder to work out which route to follow as the banknotes sank slowly out of sight. Mr Fredericks started to lag behind, and more and more often Art and Meg had to wait for him to catch them up. He had a cigarette lighter which gave a small, weak flame.

'I think we're nearly there,' Meg said

eventually, as they waited again for Mr Fredericks to reach them. He was a long way behind, the tiny spluttering flame of his lighter dancing pathetically along the tunnel wall as he staggered slowly towards them. 'I remember this bit,' Meg explained.

Art was straining to try to see the next pale hint of paper. He had the oil lamp held up almost to the ceiling, so that its light reached as far as possible along the tunnel. He turned to see what Meg was pointing at.

It was a hole in the wall – a ragged tear in the brickwork where darkness and crumbling earth spilled into the tunnel. 'This whole place is falling apart,' he said. 'But I can't see the next five-pound note.'

'That's because it's in my pocket,' Meg said.

'What?'

She sighed and folded her arms. 'The hole, here in the wall. It's where I fell and my arm went through. Don't you remember?'

'When we first found the trail.' He nodded, excited. 'Which means we're almost back at the entrance, if you're right.'

'Of course I'm right. The trail ends and

there's a hole in the wall. Besides,' she went on sullenly, 'I remember it exactly.'

'Let's hope we can find the way back from here,' Art said. 'Come on,' he called to Mr Fredericks. 'We're almost there. It's just a hundred yards or so.'

At this news, Mr Fredericks increased his pace. He was finding it difficult to push through the water and was evidently almost exhausted. In one hand he held his lighter, the other hand felt along the tunnel wall.

'We know where we are now,' Meg told him.

'Thank goodness,' Mr Fredericks gasped as he reached them. He closed his lighter and put it away in his jacket pocket. 'Give me just a moment or two to catch my breath.'

'Of course,' Art said. The relief was making him feel almost light-headed.

'I hope Jonny and Flinch are all right,' Meg said quietly, and in an instant Art's light-headedness was gone.

'Come on,' he said. 'You can rest for as long as you like once we're out of here. It's not far.'

Mr Fredericks nodded, his shadow bobbing in sympathy on the broken wall. But as he took a step forwards, his foot seemed to slip from under him and he crashed sideways.

Instinctively, Art reached out to catch his arm. But he was too late. The man was already off balance and falling. His shoulder caught Meg and sent her spinning away. Art heard the splash and the cry as she fell into the darkness behind him.

But his attention was all on Mr Fredericks crashing into the side of the tunnel, close to the point where Meg's arm had broken through the brickwork. The whole wall seemed to sag as the old man hit it. A shower of fine dust fell into Art's hair. He shook his head in annoyance and surprise, feeling the gritty powder also on his face and in his eyes.

Mr Fredericks was trying to stand up again, pushing himself off the wall. But the whole tunnel seemed to buckle under his weight and his hands were slipping off bricks as they fell away. He was scrabbling for a hold, desperately trying to save himself.

More powder now. And stones too – chunks of mortar splashing into the water all round Art. A thunderstorm of debris falling from the roof of the tunnel.

Then the first brick fell, depth-charging the water between Art and Mr Fredericks.

'Look out!' Art reached for the man's outstretched hand, hoping to pull him away as the wall finally collapsed. But he could hardly see through the falling masonry now. Mr Fredericks's hand disappeared behind a landslide of bricks and a moment later Art felt himself grabbed from behind and dragged clear.

He fell backwards with Meg. For a second his head was submerged, then he broke free to shake the water from his eyes – in time to see a whole section of the tunnel roof collapse in a fury of smoke-like dust in front of him. A fragment of brick whipped at his cheek. Meg screamed as she rose out of the water, yelling at him to get off her.

When the dust had settled and the noise had stopped ringing in their ears, Art and Meg found they were staring at a ragged pile of broken bricks and cement that completely blocked the tunnel ahead of them – the tunnel that led back to the storm drain and the way out.

'Sounded like thunder,' Jonny said.

He and Flinch were standing at a point where

three tunnels met. The wall of one of the tunnels did not reach right to the roof and a patch of light was visible at the top of the bricks, illuminating a shelf.

They listened for a few more moments, but the sound had died away.

'If it rains,' Flinch said, 'will the water rise?'

Jonny had not considered this. 'I suppose so,' he admitted. 'A bit anyway. All the more reason to see if we can get out up there.' He pointed at the strip of light. 'Doesn't look like a storm, it's sunlight.'

The torch was practically useless, its light was now so weak. He stuffed it into his coat pocket and reached up as high as he could, just managing to hook his fingertips over the top of the wall and on to the shelf.

'Can you give me a shove up?'

Flinch got behind him and pushed as Jonny pulled himself upwards. There was just enough headroom for him to be able to roll up and on to the top of the wall. The area was barely wide enough to support him. But what he found was disappointing.

In Jonny's imagination he had found a hole

like the storm drain that they could simply climb through and get back above ground. But the light was not shining, as he had hoped, through a vent in the roof. At the back edge of the shelf, the wall continued upwards for another couple of feet. But it still stopped shy of the curved ceiling.

There was another opening at the top of the dividing wall, even more narrow, into a tunnel beyond. Jonny could see the vaulted roof, where sunlight streamed through a barred opening. But the bars looked rusted and brittle. Perhaps they could be broken – if only he could squeeze through the gap between the roof of the tunnel and the dividing wall. Flinch would manage easily, but he doubted she would be able to break or bend the bars. No, he would have to try it himself, Jonny decided.

He called down to Flinch to let her know what he had found, then stretched his arms out through the narrow gap. So far, so good. By twisting his head sideways he could just get it between the wall and the ceiling. But the curvature of the roof meant he could not turn it back to see into the next tunnel. As he pushed further forward, his chest scraped against the top of the wall. And jammed.

He pushed hard, feeling his ribs tighten under the pressure. He exhaled and pushed forward another half an inch. But the pain was almost unbearable, and when he had to draw breath again his chest would expand as his lungs took in air and then the pain would get worse. Disappointed and bruised, Jonny pulled back. But he could not move. He was stuck.

Jonny's heart was pounding with the effort and the pain and the fear. He could be trapped here for ever, if he wasn't crushed by his own need for oxygen. He pulled again, but still could not move. He twisted desperately, trying to lever the top half of his body out of the narrow slot. Still nothing.

'Flinch,' he gasped. 'Flinch!' His voice was barely a croak, and there was a rushing sound in his ears that made it sound even fainter.

Then there was a scrabbling and shuffling behind him, and Jonny knew – knew for certain – that he would remain stuck here for the rest of his life, unable to get free. He was choking now, his rasping coughs sending brick dust up into his eyes and making him choke even more. Every movement was fiery pain. He wondered how long he would have to starve before he lost enough weight and size to struggle free. Would he still have the strength then? Or would he die of thirst before that? Then someone – or something – grabbed him round the waist and wrenched him out of the narrow gap.

Immediately he was free, Jonny ignored the scraping pain and rolled away from the monster, almost toppling over the edge of the shelf.

'You all right, Jonny?'

The monster that had grabbed him was Flinch, who was gazing at him in concern. The diffuse sunlight was shining on her face, glistening on the tear-tracks down her cheeks. 'I'm sorry. Thought you were stuck or something.' She turned away. 'Sorry if I hurt you.'

'No, Flinch.' He fought to get his breath back and crawled over to her. 'You were right, I was stuck. I thought I was stuck there for ever. You saved me, Flinch.'

'Saved you?' Her voice brightened and she grinned at him. 'You all right?' she asked again.

'Bit bruised. Grazed.' He made an effort to grin back. 'Fine now, thanks to you.' He rubbed at his chest. The pain was dulling to an ache. 'I think there's a way out – you can see the sunlight. But I can't get through.' He shook his head. 'We'll have to keep looking, I'm afraid. Maybe we can find a way to get to the tunnel on the other side.'

The tops of the bricks had crumbled away where Jonny had wrenched free of their grip. 'We might be able to make the gap bigger,' he murmured, rubbing at the crumbling wall. 'But we'd need a hammer of something…'

Flinch was more interested in the space between the wall and the roof. 'You're too big to get through there,' she said. 'That's obvious.'

'It's obvious *now*,' Jonny agreed.

'But I can get through,' she told him. 'Easy.'

He nodded thoughtfully. 'But can you get through those bars?'

Flinch shrugged. 'I can try. Out through the drain or whatever it is the sun's shining in. Then I can get help and come back for you.' She was already pushing her head through and looking up at the roof beyond for the source of the sunlight. When Jonny did not answer, she pulled her head back through and looked at him. 'Unless you'd rather I stayed with you,' she said.

Jonny reached out and tousled her long hair. 'Of course I'd rather we stayed together. But we have to get out of here, and if you can get through there, then that's best for us both, isn't it?'

She bit her lip and nodded. 'I'll be quick. Honest, Jonny. I can't run as quick as you, but I'll run my best.'

'Course you will.'

Arms ahead of her, as Jonny had tried, Flinch pulled herself through the gap. Jonny watched her shuffle slowly forwards until just her legs were sticking out of the hole.

'You be careful,' he warned. 'Can you reach up to the bars and break through?'

'Think so,' came the muffled reply.

'I expect there's a ledge the other side, same as here. See if you can get on to that.'

Flinch started to say something in reply. But the words turned into a scream as her legs disappeared in a sudden flurry of movement. A second later there was a dull thud from the other side of the wall.

At once, Jonny had his face pressed to the opening. 'Flinch? Flinch, what's happening? Are you all right?'

On the other side of the wall, Flinch uncurled and picked herself up. She had landed on something soft, luckily. There was no equivalent ledge on this side of the wall and the tunnel floor was much lower. It was the end of the tunnel, a dead end blocked off by the dividing wall. The narrow gap she had fallen from while trying to reach the barred opening above was fifteen feet above her head.

In the dusty sunlight that shone down into the tunnel, Flinch could see that there was no way she was ever going to be able to reach the top of the wall. The bricks here were closely knit and in better condition. She jumped desperately, but of course got nowhere close. She tried to scramble up the wall, but it was too smooth and she got no more than a few feet off the ground before sliding back down again with grazed knees and sore fingers.

'Oh, Jonny, I'm stuck,' she wailed, trying desperately not to cry.

'Don't worry, Flinch,' his voice floated back. 'Don't panic.'

'But what do I do?'

'There must be some way we can meet up again. If we keep calling to each other we can find another gap or an opening where the tunnels join.'

Flinch was looking round now, calmer but still worried and afraid. What she saw made her stomach lurch and she gave a cry of surprise and fear.

'What is it, Flinch? What's happening?'

'I thought that blanket might be part of a nest,' she said, voice shaking. 'But it wasn't. This is.'

The floor of the tunnel was strewn with debris. She had fallen on to a pile of shredded material – it looked like old clothes and curtains, dust-sheets and linen. The glassy eyes of a dead cat caught the falling sunlight and seemed to glow.

'Jonny…' Flinch's voice was barely more than a murmur. 'Jonny, I'm scared.'

Above her, Flinch could see a thin arm poking through the top of the wall and a hand waved. 'It's all right, Flinch, I'm right here. Can you see me?'

She nodded. 'Yes,' she managed to say, loud enough, she hoped, for Jonny to hear. 'I can see you waving.' Flinch waved back, though she knew he could not see her. She stood watching Jonny's arm moving back and forth above her, out of reach at the top of the blank wall that closed off the tunnel.

As she watched, Flinch became aware of a noise. It was a rhythmic, even sound that seemed to keep pace with the movement of the arm. Except it was coming from behind her, from back down the tunnel.

Slowly, she turned towards the sound. The sunlight struggled along the tunnel for several yards before it faded to shadows and darkness. And it was from the darkness that the sound was coming. A gentle, soft sound like the breeze. It reminded Flinch of something.

Then she realised that it reminded her of someone's breathing, and the monster stepped out of the shadows. Its slimy fur glistened in the weak sunlight and its massive head swung slowly upwards so that its deep, dark eyes were staring right at her. Flinch screamed, her voice deafening in the enclosed space. She backed away, right to the wall. She could hear Jonny shouting, but had no idea what he was saying. All her attention was fixed on the huge paw that reached out, claws clicking on the tunnel floor as the monster launched itself towards her.

With an involuntary shriek of fright, Arthur turned and ran. The dark shape behind him gave a roar of anger and he could hear it dragging itself over the pile of animals. Moments later, he heard the sound of claws scraping on the concrete floor. It was loud even above his laboured breathing and the blood thumping in his ears.

The low ceiling of the tunnel caught at his hair and Arthur bent lower as he ran. As he rounded the corner, he could see the rectangle of artificial light from the street above, where they had moved the cover. Grandad was still sitting at the bottom of the ladder. He turned slowly towards Arthur as he heard him approach.

'What is it?' Grandad's voice was cracked and hoarse. His eyes widened as he saw what was behind Arthur. With a startled cry, he struggled to his feet.

'Up the ladder – quick,' Arthur shouted. His voice seemed lost in the pounding of his feet and his heart. But Grandad nodded and put a foot on the bottom rung.

Arthur risked a look over his shoulder as he ran. There was something close behind him — something large and dark and covered in short, coarse hair. It had claws that gleamed on the ends of the huge paws that were propelling it along the tunnel. Its eyes were deep, dark pools that seemed to be fixed on Arthur. He turned away, running even faster, despite the tightness in his chest.

As he turned, it seemed to Arthur that for a split moment he was running down a curving tunnel lined with bricks rather than the rectangle of cement and concrete. The wires and cables had gone and his feet were splashing through dark, brackish water. Dust sprinkled from the crumbling roof and he ducked even lower. But then the impression had gone and he was back in the present.

Grandad was only on the second rung. It was an obvious effort for him to climb, his face was contorted with the effort. There was no way, Arthur realised, that Grandad would get to the top of the ladder before Arthur reached him. No way that Arthur could follow before the creature close behind caught up with him.

He could see that Grandad knew this too. The old man was leaning out from the ladder, making no attempt now to climb to the next rung. He seemed to be fumbling inside his jacket. As Arthur reached the bottom of the ladder, his grandfather was climbing back down, one hand holding the rung above and taking his weight. In the other hand, he held the knife he had used to lever up the manhole cover.

Next to the claws and teeth of the creature facing them, the knife looked rather inadequate. Grandad angled it so that it caught the light from above and reflected it into the monster's eyes. It had stopped perhaps six feet from them – close enough to lunge and strike if and when it wanted. But it seemed to shy away from the knife, at least for now.

It was like a huge rat, slimy fur slicked back and dark eyes gleaming hungrily. The creature almost filled the tunnel. Its paws were extended in front of it and the broken remnants of claws scratched at the floor impatiently. But while the overall impression was of a rodent – small, dark eyes, fur, the blunt stub of a nose – there was something almost human about the creature's features. Its nose wrinkled and wire-like whiskers twitched as it watched Arthur, and Grandad, and the knife.

'Where did it come from?' Arthur breathed, scarcely daring to speak. He started to back away down the tunnel, Grandad beside him.

'Perhaps there were two of them all the time,' Grandad suggested. 'I think it's hungry.'

A line of viscous spittle was falling from the creature's mouth. It took a scratching step after them.

'Two of them,' Arthur echoed, a memory occurring to him. 'That's it. That was what you meant before, wasn't it? That man, the one Flinch and Meg both saw talking to Mr Fredericks, he spoke of sending another one in to find the first.'

'And its been down here ever since,' Grandad agreed. 'Still looking. Conditioned – programmed, you might say – not to leave the tunnels until its task is complete.'

'No wonder it's upset.' Arthur took another step backwards. The creature was matching them step for step. It was under the open cover now, the light absorbed by its dark fur. The creature's head swung from side to side as it looked from Arthur to his grandfather and back again. As if deciding which to attack first.

'Can we outrun it?' Arthur wondered.

'I certainly can't. Jonny might have done, but I doubt that you could, young man.'

'And it's between us and the way out.'

It was gathering itself, drawing back, ready to leap at one of them.

'The knife won't stop it,' Grandad said.

But Arthur wasn't thinking about the knife. He was pulling urgently at the casebook in his pocket, but it was snagged on the pocket's lining. If only he could *remember*.

'How did you stop the other one?' Arthur asked. 'Back in 1936 – how did you kill it?'

His attention was all on the creature as it seemed to rear up, its head crooked against the roof of the tunnel as it prepared to lunge forwards. But he could sense Grandad looking at him.

'Don't you remember?' Grandad said. 'We didn't want to kill it.'

Chapter 9

From the ledge on the other side of the wall, Jonny could not see what was happening. But he could hear Flinch's cries for help, could hear the heavy breathing and the scratching progress of the monster. By angling his head, he caught glimpses of Flinch's hands as she leaped and scrabbled in an effort to reach the opening at the top of the wall. And he could see that she was not even close.

In frustration, Jonny hammered at the bricks with his fists. He wanted to scream out in anger and frustration. Somehow the pain of thumping the coarse bricks made him feel better, as if he was suffering with Flinch. Then one of the bricks moved.

He thought he had imagined it at first. He thumped at it again – and yes, it definitely shifted, just a fraction. It was in the top layer of the wall and, by angling himself on the ledge, Jonny found he could swing his legs round and kick at it.

The third kick jarred his leg right up to his thigh. His heel ached. But the brick shifted, skewing sideways and sending mortar crumbling.

He hauled himself round and grabbed at the brick, tearing it free from the wall.

'Hang on, Flinch,' he yelled. 'Just hang on. I'm coming.'

But even as he wrenched the next brick free and started on a third, he knew that however quickly he could make a gap large enough to squeeze through, he would be too late.

The top of the wall was simply too high for Flinch to reach. Terror and determination combined to help her scramble halfway to the narrow line of blackness where she knew Jonny was waiting. But after that her momentum slowed and she could not hold on to the sheer wall any longer. She dropped back to the tunnel floor, bruised and battered and crying, but desperate to try again.

After three attempts, she knew she was never going to make it. She could hear Jonny shouting that he was coming to help, but while she trusted him completely, she knew that really there was no way he could get to her in time. She was trapped with the monster.

Accepting this, she turned to face it. The light from the drain illuminated the creature as it made its slow progress towards her. She could see the glistening wet hair that covered its body, the huge paws tipped with claws that scratched at the tunnel floor as it moved. The dark eyes gleamed, seeming to attract the light and then reflect it. A narrow mouth opened just enough to reveal yellowed teeth that clicked as they bit together. It was like an enormous rat, except that the face seemed more expressive than any rat Flinch had seen.

The creature leaned its head to one side as it watched her. Somehow that seemed to make the monster less threatening. Flinch could remember feeding the stub end of a mouldy piece of cheese to a rat back in the Cannoniers' old den, before it was taken over by the strange puppet exhibition. That was the way the rat had looked at her as she held out the food – as if not quite sure what to make of it. As if deciding what it should do.

Except that now, Flinch thought, *she* was the food the monster was considering. As she realised this, the creature lifted its head and started down the tunnel again, its mind apparently made up.

With a shriek, Flinch turned back to the wall and leaped at it. She grabbed and scrabbled as high as she could, fingers grazed and torn as she tried to get a handhold. She managed to work the fingers of one hand into the gap between two bricks where the mortar had perished. She pulled, her whole weight painfully on the fingers, feet kicking out to try to get a grip.

Glancing down, she could see that the monster was right below her. Its head was level with her feet. If she fell – *when* she fell – she would land right in front of it. Right by its head… its mouth…

Above her, Jonny was still shouting. She looked up and a stream of sharp dust sprinkled into her face. She coughed and blinked and shook her head to try to get it out of her eyes. But already she could feel her fingers slipping, could feel her toes skid across the wall. And she could hear the snarl of the creature below. She could see it rearing up on its back legs and almost taste the rancid breath as the massive head came level with her feet. Its snout brushed against her leg and Flinch screamed.

Jonny had managed to remove the top layer of bricks from a section of the wall. The gap was bigger, but still it was just too small. He froze at the sound of Flinch's scream, then grabbed one of the bricks he had knocked free and started to hammer at the next row.

Immediately the first brick moved. But even above the sound of Flinch's shrieking, Jonny heard the metallic clang. The brick was loose now, but it seemed to be jammed. He managed to prise it free with his finger, wriggling it out of the wall. But then he saw what had made the noise, what had held the brick in place.

There was a thick metal pipe running through the wall, lying across the top of the next layer of bricks and embedded in the mortar. He could get the bricks out, he knew that now, but the pipe was another matter. If he could neither bend nor break it, he would need to remove another whole section of the wall to make enough room to crawl through *under* the pipe. That would take for ever.

Even as he realised this, Flinch's screaming stopped and everything was suddenly still and silent.

Somewhere deep in the tunnels, Art and Meg could hear the sound. They stared at each other in the near-darkness, frozen.

'That was Flinch,' Meg said as the scream suddenly cut out.

Art nodded. The sound echoed all around them, so that it was impossible to tell which direction it had come from. But it had seemed to Art that it was louder to his side, where a narrow tunnel fed into the one they had been following.

'This way,' Art said.

'You sure?'

She would know if he lied. But Art wouldn't lie to Meg anyway. 'No,' he said. 'But I think it came from down here.'

'Then what are we waiting for?'

Flinch was so surprised that she stopped screaming. The creature had pushed itself up on to its hind legs, standing upright. It pushed its head gently upwards, nudging her. It was the feel of the creature's head on her legs, the smell and sound of its breath, that had made Flinch scream.

But now the creature was supporting her. Flinch was sitting on its snout as it scrabbled at the wall to raise itself to its full height. It was lifting her gently, carefully, up the wall – helping her to reach the top. In surprise more than fear,

Flinch held on to the warm wet nose. What she had taken for a snarl now sounded more like the purring of a cat.

The wall was still too high. Even with the creature at full stretch, Flinch was a couple of feet short of the top. The creature too seemed to realise this and it lowered her gently to the ground, before flopping back on to its front paws and backing away. Its eyes were wide as if in apology.

Flinch stared at the creature. She no longer thought of it as a monster. After a moment she took a step towards it and reached out gingerly. The creature did not move, though its eyes followed her hand. Gently, Flinch patted it on the nose. It did not seem to object and lowered its head as if inviting her to pat that as well. So she did.

'Thanks, Ratty,' she said. 'It was a good try. But I think we're still stuck down here.'

Meg stopped so suddenly that Art almost walked into her.

'What is it?'

She started down the tunnel again. 'It's Flinch,' she said, sounding surprised.

Over Meg's shoulder, Art could see a faint light shining down from above. The tunnel roof seemed to be higher ahead of them and there was a wall – a dead end. But in front of the wall, clearly visible in the faint light from outside, was Flinch. And with her was the monster.

As they approached, the huge creature twisted round in the tunnel. Its eyes flashed and Art caught a brief glimpse of teeth protruding from the dark fur of its face.

'No!' Flinch called, and Art realised with surprise that she was talking to the monster. 'They're friends of mine. It's all right.'

The creature turned slowly back to face Flinch.

'They won't hurt you,' she said gently, stroking the monster's face.

Art and Meg stood staring in amazement.

'Hello,' Flinch said. Her coat was filthy and torn, her face was almost black with dirt and her long hair was hanging limp and bedraggled across her shoulders in wet bunches. But she was grinning. 'This is Ratty,' she said.

'Where's Jonny?' Art asked as they hesitantly edged round the creature. He was not sure what else to say.

Flinch pointed to the wall behind her. 'Through there,' she said. 'There's a gap at the top of the wall into the next tunnel. I fell through and its too small for Jonny.'

'Jonny?' Art shouted.

The creature – Ratty – drew back at the sound of Art's voice, but Flinch stroked and patted it.

'Up here,' Jonny's voice came back, and Art could see a pale arm waving at the top of the wall. 'I'm trying to widen the gap so I can get through. Maybe I can help you all back up here and we can reach the drain.'

'Good idea,' Meg said. 'We found the way out again, but the tunnel's blocked. So that may be the only way.'

'There's a pipe I can't shift. I need to get under it, I think. Might take a while.'

Art gave a nervous laugh. 'We're not going anywhere.'

'Art?'

'Yes, Jonny?'

'I can't see into the tunnel,' Jonny told them. 'So tell me, what *is* going on down there?'

* * *

The morning was crisp and chilly. Two men stood at the edge of the storm drain on the waste ground behind Mr Fredericks's house.

'You're sure he's not back?' Sergeant Drake asked.

'I haven't seen him,' Constable Atkins replied. 'He was supposed to get the kids home, then report back here. But that was hours ago.'

Drake nodded. Wilkins had returned almost immediately to say that the children – Art and Meg – were climbing down into the culvert. And Drake had sent him back to haul them out and take them home. But for the last few hours his mind had been on the murder inquiry and on searching the house. There were things here that did not make sense, at least not yet.

'He's not gone back to the station, I suppose.'

'No, sir. And I took the liberty of checking your house too. Your Arthur isn't at home. He might have left for school…' Atkins shrugged. 'Bit early, though. Was when I was there, anyway.'

'So you think they're still down here?'

Atkins considered, blowing out a long steamy breath. 'I think it's worth a look, sir.'

'All right.' Drake sighed. 'Kids, I don't know.

Give me a hand down, will you?'

They sat in the tunnel and listened to the steady thump of Jonny hammering at the bricks above them. At least it was dry here, Art thought. He looked round at the debris scattered over the ground. A yard-long section of branch from a tree had somehow been swept into the mess, the leaves curled and brittle.

Art had tried to lift Flinch high enough to reach the top of the wall, but he was no taller than the creature had been on its hind legs. They had no choice but to wait for Jonny to widen the gap. Then perhaps he could reach down to them.

It might be a long wait, Art knew. Jonny had warned them that the bricks were in better condition and the cement stronger in the section of wall under the pipe. It was slow going and there seemed to be an age now between Jonny's reports that he had successfully removed another brick.

'You could try breaking the pipe,' Meg had suggested.

'Yeah,' Jonny called back. 'And get drenched. It might flood the tunnel.'

'Maybe then we could float out,' Meg told him.

'Could we really?' Flinch asked.

'I doubt it,' Art told her. 'The water wouldn't rise high enough. It would just run off down the tunnels. And, depending on the pressure in the pipe and how big it is, it might sweep us off with it.'

Flinch nodded solemnly. 'I don't know if Ratty can swim,' she said.

'He's coped down here well enough.' Art risked patting the creature's head, and was surprised at how warm it was. He had not expected it to feel like an animal at all, but cold and slimy and damp. In fact, it reminded him of patting the milkman's horse.

'I guess he eats rats,' Meg said, looking round at the debris on the floor of the tunnel. 'And cats when he can get them.'

'He's got to eat something,' Flinch protested. 'I wasn't blaming him.'

'That must be why the rats came out of the drain,' Art said thoughtfully. 'You remember we heard about what happened at Mrs Briggson's.'

'Happened to us too,' Flinch said. 'That's why we had to come down the drain, to escape all the rats at Mr Fredericks's house.'

'Mr Fredericks, yes,' he said slowly, as he remembered what had happened to the man. 'He was down here too.' Then, with a cold shock, he remembered where they had met him and what else they had found. He looked at Flinch as she stroked the huge creature's head and cooed at it. It seemed so docile, so tame...

'Flinch,' Art said quietly. 'Just be careful, won't you?'

'He's all right. He just kills rats and stuff for food. When he has too. It's not surprising they're scared and run away from him. But you can see he's friendly.'

'He seems to be,' Meg agreed.

'He does now,' Art told them. 'But you're forgetting, Meg. However calm that thing seems at the moment, we found a dead policeman in the tunnels.'

Meg's eyes were wide as she remembered. She leaped away from the creature and huddled close to Art. 'Flinch,' she hissed, 'Art's right. It might be tame now, but it's a killer. Get over here, quick.'

Flinch was frowning at them. 'You don't know that Ratty did it,' she said. 'He wouldn't. He

176

couldn't. I know he couldn't.'

'It does seem hard to believe.' Art was trying to keep his voice quiet and calm, so as not to alarm or startle the creature. 'But I really can't see that there's any other explanation. There's nothing and nobody else down here that could have done it.'

'I'm afraid you're wrong about that.' The voice was measured and confident. It came from down the tunnel, just beyond the light from the drain above. 'And there's a very simple explanation for the dead policeman.'

Art was on his feet, struggling to see who was speaking. A dark figure stepped forward into the edge of the light. It was Mr Fredericks. But a very different Mr Fredericks from the nervous, diffident man they were used to. Although his clothes were filthy and covered in grey dust from where the tunnel had collapsed, he was standing with an assurance and bearing that made him seem taller than Art remembered.

'The girl's right, of course,' Mr Fredericks said, striding down the tunnel towards them.

The creature seemed to shy away from the sound of his voice, drawing itself into a tight ball and keeping close to Flinch.

'That creature didn't kill the policeman,' Mr Fredericks explained calmly. '*I* did.'

Atkins had brought a lantern. Its pallid light was broken by the jagged pile of bricks and concrete that blocked the tunnel ahead of them.

Sergeant Drake pulled away some of the loose debris, but when he tried to shift the larger chunks of concrete and the sections of roof and wall that had fallen intact, he could not even begin to move them.

Balancing the lantern on the edge of the rubble, Atkins went to help him. But still they could not shift it.

'Probably as well, sir,' Atkins said. 'We might bring the whole roof down on top of us.'

'There's no way of knowing how recent this fall is,' Drake decided. He dusted his hands off on his jacket and gave a snort of annoyance at the mess he was making. 'But they can't have got through there.'

'And if they went through before it fell? Or if...' Atkins stopped, and retrieved the lantern.

Drake knew what he had left unsaid. What if

Wilkins and the children – including his son – were underneath the fallen rubble. 'Let's just hope they aren't in there somewhere,' he said. 'Because if they are, there's no way on earth that we can get to them through here.'

They turned and made their way back towards the storm drain.

Jonny was holding his breath. He strained to hear what Mr Fredericks was saying. It had taken him a moment to recognise the voice. Even now as he listened, he found it hard to believe that this was the same man they had found whimpering over his dead cat. Except, of course, Jonny was sure now that it was not his cat at all.

'I was hoping that the Invisible Detective himself could be persuaded to help me find this abomination.' Jonny assumed he meant the creature that he could not see. He could hear, though – the snuffling of its breath and its claws as they scratched at the tunnel floor. 'But if Brandon Lake decides to send his juvenile colleagues, that's fine by me. It is, after all, results that count.'

As Mr Fredericks spoke, Jonny started again

on the wall. He kept as quiet as he could, pulling at the bricks with all his might rather than thumping at them. He was not sure if Mr Fredericks knew he was there or not, but there was no point in advertising the fact. Now that he had removed several layers of bricks below the pipe, the others moved more easily. He pulled another one free in a silent shower of aged cement.

Art's first thought was that there had been an accident of some sort. Somehow the policeman had died and Mr Fredericks was blaming himself.

Meg seemed to be thinking along the same lines. 'You wanted the Invisible Detective to find this creature? To stop it killing more cats like Tiger?'

Mr Fredericks laughed at that. He threw his head back and laughed so loud that the sound reverberated round the tunnels and the creature drew back in fright. 'You think I care about a few cats? It can kill as many cats as it likes. No.' He was regaining his composure now. 'No, I wanted it back because the people I…' He paused, as if to find the right word. 'The people I borrowed it from want it back. Which is a shame,' he admitted.

'The way the thing can burrow through the walls of the tunnels and force open metal doors is so very useful.'

'What do you mean, useful?' Art did not like the way the conversation was going at all. He could see that Meg was also apprehensive, gnawing at her bottom lip. Flinch was absorbed in trying to comfort Ratty. 'What walls? What doors?' But even as he spoke, he realised what Mr Fredericks meant. 'The bank!'

'That's right.' The man had taken a few steps towards them. He seemed to be examining the broken branch that was jammed against the side of the tunnel. 'You found some of the notes. But most of them are still safe and sound, together with the other items of interest that the creature helped me to retrieve. The next tunnel along runs right past the vault. Right into it now,' he added with a chuckle.

'What about your brother?' Meg asked abruptly. 'Did it kill him?'

Mr Fredericks was stooping to pick up the branch. He paused and looked at her in surprise. 'I have no brother,' he said. 'I don't know what you mean.'

But Art did. 'The old man. The police identified the body of an old man as a Mr Fredericks who lived off St Swithin's Lane.'

'Ah, yes, Mr Fredericks. The *real* Mr Fredericks.' He lifted the branch. Dead, dry leaves rustled and broke free, falling like burnt paper to the floor. 'I needed an address where the Invisible Detective could contact me and a name I could use. The late Mr Fredericks was kind enough to supply both.' He held up the branch, apparently admiring it. 'At a price, of course. Everything has a price.'

Art's throat was tight and dry. 'You killed him.'

Mr Fredericks – or whatever his name really was – shrugged. 'Everything dies eventually.' He made it sound light and casual. 'Just look at this branch.'

'But we found you with Tiger,' Flinch said. She was staring across from the other side of the frightened creature. Its dark eyes were intent on the branch, on the man's movements.

'I was expecting Brandon Lake himself to make further enquiries. I knew my friend here was killing cats for food, scaring rats out of the sewers.

182

But all my attempts to find him had failed. I heard you outside the house that day when you were kind and naïve enough to visit me.' He lowered the branch and his face crumpled into an exaggerated mask of sadness and despair. 'Oh, my poor Tiger,' he sobbed theatrically. 'The nasty monster has hurt my poor ickle Tiger-Wiger.' Then suddenly he was back to his serious, unpleasant self. 'And you fell for it. How pathetic.'

Above him, Art could hear the scraping and muffled thumping as Jonny continued to attack the wall. He did not know what Mr Fredericks intended, but if Jonny could break through to them at least they would have another chance of escape, however slight. He glanced up and could see the dust produced by Jonny's efforts spiralling lazily down like smoke.

Except that some of it *was* smoke. Art turned quickly back to Mr Fredericks and saw that he had produced a lighter from his pocket. Its small flame danced lazily, flickering in the slight breeze.

'So we've found this creature for you,' Art said. He wanted to keep Mr Fredericks talking, to buy as much time as he could for Jonny. 'If it's as clever as you say, it can dig us out of here – it can clear the rubble where the tunnel's collapsed.'

'You know, that's a very good idea,' Mr Fredericks admitted. 'It might well do that.'

'So we can get out,' Meg said. She glanced warily at Art. Her expression was unreadable, but he could see that her eyes were wide with worry.

'We?' Mr Fredericks laughed again. 'Oh, no. I don't think so. Such a shame,' he went on, taking another step towards them and raising the lighter towards the dry branch. 'The Invisible Detective's juvenile accomplices did such a good job of helping his client, and yet none of them can be allowed to live to tell their story.' He shook his head in mock sadness.

'What are you going to do?' Art found he was backing away. He and Meg and Flinch were all huddled close to the creature now. The animal seemed the most scared of all of them. It shied away, making soft whimpering sounds.

'Come here.' Mr Fredericks's voice was severe. He touched the lighter to the end of the branch. 'I said come here, you revolting thing.'

The branch burst into flames immediately. A

brittle crackling accompanied the leaping yellow of the fire. Shadows flickered into smoky life on the tunnel walls and the smell clawed at the back of Art's throat.

The creature had drawn away from Mr Fredericks when he first spoke. But now, with the fire, it seemed to collapse in fear and shuffled slowly away from Flinch and towards the man.

Flinch made to follow, reaching out to stroke and comfort Ratty. But Meg grabbed her hand and pulled her back. The young girl gave a sob of frustration.

'Oh, how touching.' Mr Fredericks had the blazing branch raised high above his head. It almost reached the raised roof of this area of sewer. 'That makes it all the more sad.'

'What?' Meg demanded, the light and shadows from the fire emphasising her anger.

'That you have to die,' Mr Fredericks said simply. 'I trained this abomination, you know. It really does understand what you say to it. I trained it to obey my every wish. Trained it with fire.' He thrust the branch towards the creature to punctuate his words, and it shied away, its eyes glowing black with reflected light. With his free hand, Mr Fredericks roughly shoved the creature's head away so that it turned back towards Art and Meg and Flinch. He held the burning wood close to the creature's face and Art could see the terror in its eyes. He could see that whatever Mr Fredericks told it to do, it would obey without hesitation rather than face his anger.

Mr Fredericks was laughing again. His lips were curled into a devilish grin of anticipation. 'Go on, then,' he snarled at the creature. 'Kill them.'

Arthur pushed his grandfather one way and then he leaped the other. The creature crashed between them with a savage roar of anger. Arthur was more concerned he might have hurt Grandad. But he could see the old man pulling himself to his feet.

The creature was scrabbling to gain a purchase on the concrete floor, struggling to twist round in the confined space. Arthur reached out and grabbed Grandad's arm, pulling him back down the tunnel towards the ladder. There would still not be time to climb up, but at least the creature was not between them and the way out.

One of the claws struck the ground so hard that a spark shot out. Then the thing was moving again. It seemed even larger now, as if its hair was standing on end in anger. It gave a furious snarl and started towards them, but slowly and cautiously. Its dark eyes were fixed on Arthur as he reached the ladder and stood below the open cover. Perhaps it was wary of the light from outside. Living in the tunnels for so long, it must be used to the dark.

Fire. Somewhere on the tip of his memory was something to do with fire. Arthur looked round frantically, but there was nothing in the tunnel that would burn – even if he had a way to ignite it. There was just bare concrete and the cables. And all they had was a knife.

Cables. The creature's claws clicked on the ground and it stalked closer. Closer.

'Any bright ideas?' Grandad asked. His voice was surprisingly calm.

'I'm not sure,' Arthur admitted. He had the beginnings of an idea. But he needed to think it through.

'If not, then I suggest I hold it off with the knife

while you get up that ladder.'

'No way,' Arthur said fiercely. 'It'll kill you.'

'Better than killing both of us, surely.'

'Give me the knife.' Arthur held out his hand. The creature was so close now that he could hear its breathing, smell its rancid breath.

'You'll be quicker up the ladder,' Grandad retorted, moving the knife out of Arthur's reach. 'You'd never keep it away long enough for me to get up there.'

'I know,' Arthur told him, his teeth gritted. 'That's not what I'm doing.'

Grandad looked at him, his eyes narrowed thoughtfully. 'Then what?'

But Arthur had no time to answer. The creature was almost on them. Again it paused, gathered itself, prepared to pounce. Arthur reached across quickly and grabbed the knife, wrenching it from Grandad's grasp. As he pulled it away, Arthur swept the knife in as wide an arc as he could. He was relieved to see that the creature followed the knife's movement with its eyes and even drew back slightly. He had bought them some time – mere seconds, but that was all he needed. He hoped.

Grandad was by the ladder and Arthur was on

the other side of the tunnel, close to the opposite wall. The cables were fed through brackets at intervals along the wall, so that they hung in loops between each bracket. Arthur grabbed one of the thick cables and pulled it tight so that he was holding it in front of him. Through the insulation he could feel that it was actually a bundle of cables and wires bound together.

The creature was moving again – making for Arthur, perhaps because he had the knife or perhaps because he was at the edge of the light.

Arthur doubled the thick cable over, wrapping it round the blade. He was glad the handle of the knife was made of wood – that should mean it was insulated. As the creature roared and leaped, he ripped the blade through the cable, dropping one end immediately and jabbing forwards with the other.

Arthur's hope was that the power in the cable would spark and ignite, or at least give the creature a severe electric shock. But they were not power cables he had cut through. Instead of hot fiery current spitting from the severed end, cold light spilled out from a hundred fractured filaments. Fibre optic cables. Phone or data or television signals –

not electricity. Harmless.

But the effect on the creature was dramatic. The bunch of cables Arthur thrust towards it stopped right in front of its eyes. It blinked in surprise, then gave a howl of anguished pain and jumped back, turning its head away from the sudden intense light.

This would not keep the creature at bay for long, though. Arthur could see it already adjusting, peering back at him as its eyes got used to the light. He jabbed forward again, and again it shied away – but not so much, not so far. Not for so long.

With a speed and determination stemming from fear and desperation, Arthur grabbed another of the loops of cable. One of them must be electrical, surely it must.

Again he braced the knife against the thick insulation. Again he hacked through the cable just as the creature launched itself towards him. Again he dropped one end and thrust the other at the thing's face.

Above them, the lights in the street went out. For a moment everything was absolute blackness. Except for the glinting eyes of the creature as it erupted out of the darkness. Arthur felt the weight of it strike his arm and drive him backwards. He stumbled and fell, still holding the cable out in front of him like some magic talisman. And about as much use, he thought, as the ground crunched into the back of his head.

The pain was immediate and intense. So intense he saw bright lights in front of his eyes. And there was a sound – a terrible screeching that bit into his numbed mind and tore at his ears as the creature fell towards him.

It took Arthur several moments to realise that the lights and the sound were not inside his head. The brilliant flare of white and yellow was flashing and sparking from the end of the cable he held, and the screech was the agony of the creature. Its whole body was writhing and smoking in the flashing light.

Arthur struggled to pull himself clear, but already he knew it was no use. It was only the creature's death agonies that kept it upright. It buckled and screamed as it was jolted by the power from the cable. But it was dying, falling. It was falling towards Arthur, bringing the cable with it. Another moment and the cable would be forced back on to him, crushed between their bodies. Then the current would flow into Arthur too.

Just as the creature sagged forwards, Arthur felt the cable yanked from his grip. Moments later the full weight of the creature collapsed on top of him. He could feel its warmth, taste its breath. Its ragged breathing and erratic heartbeat seemed to join with his own until, with a low moan and a sudden shudder, they stopped.

Hands reached under Arthur's shoulders, dragging him backwards, out from under the dead weight. Both broken ends of the cable lay sparking and arcing against the tunnel wall. Grandad collapsed beside Arthur, breathing heavily.

'I just managed to get the cable out of the way in time,' he gasped.

'Thanks.'

In the irregular light of the spitting cable, Arthur could see that Grandad was smiling weakly. 'My pleasure. And thank you. That was pretty smart, you know. Just don't try it at home,' he added.

They lay for a while, catching their breath, watching the cable as it continued its lightning show on the other side of the tunnel.

'I don't remember how it ended, back in 1936,' Arthur said at last. 'I've read it, but I can't remember.

It's like I'm not meant to know that yet.'

'A variation on a theme,' Grandad said. He was struggling to get up. 'I think we had better be going. Before someone comes to find out what's happened.'

'I think we blacked out the whole area,' Arthur said. Above the manhole he could see only darkness. 'There'll be a lot of angry people up there – it's football tonight.'

Grandad laughed, and started carefully up the ladder. He made slow, ponderous progress. At the top he climbed out and then knelt down beside the open cover to help Arthur out after him. 'Back then,' he said, as Arthur emerged into the eerie stillness of the street, 'the monster was shaped like a man.'

Chapter 10

There was no way that Jonny was going to have the gap big enough to get through and help. He could hear Mr Fredericks clearly, and he tore more and more frantically at the bricks, but he knew it was useless.

So instead, Jonny turned his attention to the pipe. From the flickering, dancing shadows and the smell of the fire, he had a good idea what was going on below him on the other side of the wall. He could see dark trails of smoke curling up towards the drain above them. Getting drenched, he decided, would no longer be a concern. In fact, a large quantity of water pouring down into the tunnel below would probably help Art and Meg and Flinch.

He yanked at the pipe, feeling it bend and give. But not enough. It was set solid into the walls at either side of the ledge. He tried lying down and kicking at it, like he had with the wall. But apart from aching feet, he achieved little. He pulled at it again, looking in the murky light for a weak point – for where there was the greatest movement.

There was a joint about halfway along. It was a narrow metal collar where two sections of pipe had been welded into the slightly larger sleeve of metal. If there was a weak point, this must be it.

Down below, Jonny could hear Flinch shouting something. He could make out Art's more measured tones but was unable to pick up what he was saying. Jonny looked round desperately for something that might be of use, something he could use to help him break the pipe. But there was nothing except the broken bricks and shattered mortar from the wall. Initially he had not wanted to use a brick to hammer at the wall because of the noise it would make, but he was not worried about noise now.

Jonny picked up the nearest brick and brought it crashing down on the pipe with a heavy clang. The edge of the brick crumbled under the impact, but there was a mark on the pipe. Not much – just the smallest of dents – but enough for Jonny to believe that this might actually work. Holding the pipe firm in one hand, he hammered at it repeatedly with the brick and watched anxiously as the dent grew slowly bigger.

* * *

Meg saw the creature hesitate. It looked from the fire that Mr Fredericks held close to its face to Flinch, then back again.

'What are you waiting for?' Mr Fredericks shouted at it. 'Kill them.'

Flinch was screaming for Ratty not to listen. Art was trying to calm her, and Meg stood watching the creature's indecision. She knew it would soon make up its mind. From the obvious fear in its eyes whenever it looked at the burning branch, she knew what it would do. Above them, from where Jonny was hiding, a rhythmic clanging started. It sounded, she thought vaguely, like a blacksmith's forge.

The whole tunnel seemed to be filled with sound now. It blotted out Meg's thoughts and kept her rooted to the spot. Art's attempts to reason with Mr Fredericks and comfort Flinch. Flinch's screams and shouts. Mr Fredericks's increasingly hysterical orders to the creature, which was itself grunting and snarling as it struggled to decide what to do. And over everything the metallic ringing from whatever Jonny was doing.

It seemed to Meg that this went on for hours. Time was drawn out, elongated, like the moments on a cold morning when she knew she had to get out of her warm bed but kept putting it off. Similarly, she knew this could only have lasted a few seconds. Then, all too soon, the creature swung away from Mr Fredericks, from the fire, and stalked towards them.

Art pulled Flinch behind him. Meg too was backing away. They were tight against the tunnel wall now, with nowhere else to go. Trapped.

'There must be something here we can use to defend ourselves,' Art said. He was looking down at the ground, at the twisted remnants of sheets and broken pieces of wood. But Meg could see nothing that would be of use. The creature was almost on them.

Over its massive, shaggy shoulder Meg could see Mr Fredericks. He was holding the burning branch triumphantly, and his eyes gleamed with menace and malice.

'Yes, go on. Go on,' he hissed.

The creature paused, ready to strike. The insistent hammering from above seemed to be faster, more urgent now, as if to emphasise their increasing danger.

'Hold on, Art.' Jonny's voice was almost lost

in the sound of his work. 'I'm nearly through the pipe.'

But it was too late. Meg could see in the creature's eyes that it was about to launch itself at them. It drew back slightly as it prepared to jump.

Jonny's arm ached so much he had tried hammering with his other hand. But his aim was not so good and he had less strength in his left arm. So, despite the discomfort, he went back to his right and redoubled his efforts, ignoring the pain in his wrist, elbow and shoulder. Was that the tiniest of holes in the pipe? He could not tell in this light. But with renewed hope, he went on hammering.

Suddenly, he felt the pipe come loose. He was holding it tight in his left hand as he hammered at it with a crumbling brick, and his hand moved. The whole of the collar had split apart, the metal pulling free and unpeeling like the skin of an orange. The end of the pipe bent upwards and Jonny ducked away instinctively to avoid the sudden gushing pressure of the water he knew was about to drench him. If he could angle the pipe so the water poured down into the tunnel below, he might be in time to save his friends.

But nothing happened. There was no water. He stared at the broken end of the pipe, his vision misting and his breath suddenly short and laboured as he realised that their last hope was gone. The pipe was empty.

The creature was rearing up on its hind legs, poised to leap at them. Art was holding Flinch's arms, trying to push her behind him in an attempt to shield her for as long as possible. He could feel her struggling and trying to pull free. This was it, Art thought. He wondered, at the back of his mind, whether anyone would find their bodies. At least Jonny would be all right, if only he could find a way out of the tunnels.

Distracted by these thoughts, his hold on Flinch slackened, and suddenly she pulled away. Before Art could stop her, she stepped forward – right into the path of the creature.

For a moment it remained poised on its hind legs, its head tilted to one side as it watched Flinch. The metallic hammering suddenly stopped.

'Ratty?' she said. 'Please help us, Ratty.' Her voice was little more than a sob in the sudden stillness.

Slowly, almost gently, the creature lowered itself. It extended its neck so that its head was close to Flinch. Tentatively, she reached up and stroked its hairy cheek.

Mr Fredericks was livid. His face burned red with emotion and rage and he stepped beside the creature, squeezing into the narrow gap between monster and tunnel wall.

'Kill her, you fool,' he snarled. 'Kill her now.' He took another step forward and thrust the branch at the creature's face. It was burning low now – more smoke than flame. But the fire was still fierce enough to terrify the creature. It pulled away, its face brushing against Flinch's as it tried to avoid the flames.

Flinch grabbed the creature, wrapping her arms tightly about its neck and hugging it. She was murmuring something, but Art could not hear her above the sound of Mr Fredericks's shouts of rage and the crackling of the fire. He took a deep breath to shout to Flinch to try to push past the creature, to get to the tunnel behind and run.

But he stopped. There was something wrong. Something he could almost taste in the air.

Meg had noticed it too. 'What's that smell?' she said urgently.

From her widening eyes, Art could tell that she realised at the same moment he did. Jonny, the pipe, the smell...

Art grabbed Meg's arm and pulled her after him. He didn't care what the creature did now, wasn't worried about what Mr Fredericks was capable of doing. He saw only the burning remains of the branch and the narrowest of gaps on the opposite side of the tunnel between the creature and the wall. 'Come on!'

Together they charged at the gap. Flinch was already letting go of the creature. Its head was swinging back round, teeth bared, but not towards Art and Meg. It turned sharply, viciously, towards Mr Fredericks.

It took Jonny a while to realise his mistake. He thought the hissing sound was his own attempts to draw breath. Then it occurred to him that while he was having trouble breathing, he could smell something. A strong, pungent smell that caught at the back of his throat and clogged his lungs.

Gas.

It wasn't a water pipe at all, it was a gas pipe.

And in the tunnel on the other side of the wall there was a fire.

He tried to scream a warning, but he was choking now. He clasped his handkerchief over his nose and rolled backwards, away from the open ends of the broken pipe. Too late he realised this was a mistake. He felt his arm fall into space as he reached the edge of the shelf on which he was lying. A split second later, his whole body was off the edge and falling.

But now at least he could breathe, and he took in a huge rasping lungful of air before crashing into the shallow water in the bottom of the tunnel. His back cracked painfully on the ground, the water splashed up round him, and his head sank below the surface.

For a moment he was stunned by the impact, lying prone, still, submerged in the shallow water. And that saved his life.

Flinch fought against Art. He was trying to pull her along with them as the creature turned. Another moment and it would block the tunnel as it rounded on Mr Fredericks.

Realising the danger he was in, the man was himself now backing away. He was shouting and screaming at the creature, waving the remains of the branch in front of him. But the flames were dying. A single blackened stump of wood thrust up from the middle of the fire, a skeletal remnant of the branch.

Art managed to pull Flinch back. 'There's gas,' he shouted. 'Unless that fire goes out soon…'

But his words were whipped away by the creature's roar of anger. They turned in time to see an enormous clawed paw lash out towards Mr Fredericks. The creature was bearing down on him, snarling with pent-up rage and hatred. It struck the remains of the burning branch and sent it spinning down the tunnel. Sparks dripped from it as it Catherine-wheeled. Mr Fredericks was screaming, arms up to protect his face from the creature's jaws. Then the air itself caught fire.

The entire tunnel was a sudden curtain of orange flame as the burning branch caught the escaping cloud of gas. The fire billowed out towards Art and the others.

'Run!' Art screamed, and pushed Meg and

Flinch ahead of him down the tunnel. Could they outrun a fireball? Maybe Jonny could, on the other side of the wall. They stamped through the shallow water, heads down, arms working. Art could feel the heat at his back and glanced over his shoulder. At once he could see that the fire was catching up with them, would reach them in a moment and wash over them.

Art could almost feel the hair at the back of his neck curling in the heat when he saw the patch of darkness to their left. A side tunnel or alcove. Ahead of him, the girls were almost past it. He dived forwards, wrapping his arms round both of them and dragging them into the darkness, hoping it was not just a stain or patch of moss on the wall.

They fell together in a tangle of arms and legs, splashing into the foul-smelling water. Art turned in time to see a fiery wave sweep down the tunnel beside them and felt the heat of it on his face. He could feel his skin redden and his eyes were suddenly dry. Then, as quickly as it had come, the roaring torrent of flame and smoke was gone and the tunnel was silent save for the sound of three exhausted children trying to get their breath.

'Is that it?' Meg said between gasps. 'Is it over?'

'I'm not sure.' Art was staring down the tunnel they had fallen into. Was it his imagination or was a shadowy figure moving slowly towards them? His eyes were blurred from the glare of the fire and he blinked to try to clear them.

'Ratty?' Flinch said in a small voice. Her long hair was hanging in wet bunches across her shoulders, glistening in what light there was. 'What's happened to Ratty?'

Meg caught Art's arm as the dark figure strode towards them. Her own hair seemed even more curled now that it was wet. 'Be ready to run,' she whispered.

The figure was almost with them now and Art could see that it was smaller than he had at first thought. In fact, it was the silhouette of someone no taller than himself, and Art laughed.

'Sorry about that,' said Jonny. 'Well, I didn't know it was a gas pipe, did I?'

Together they made their way back to the creature's nest. The walls of the tunnel had been blasted clean of moss and algae by the fireball, and the bricks were blackened and coated with soot.

Jonny told them that he was under water when the fireball raced along his tunnel. He explained how, after the blast, he had managed to stuff his wet handkerchief into the open end of the pipe and hoped that would block the flow, at least for now. 'But we need to get out of here and find someone who can repair it properly,' he said.

'Or can turn off the gas,' Art suggested, practical as ever.

He made Meg smile with the matter-of-fact way he just seemed to accept the bizarre events they were caught up in. For an instant she wanted to hug him, but she folded her arms and settled for a thin smile. He would only be embarrassed, she decided.

Jonny and Art were laughing and joking, though Meg could hear the remains of their nervousness mixed in with the humour. Flinch was a different matter.

She was crouched down beside the blackened body of the creature, sobbing. Meg knelt beside her and put her arm round the girl. Flinch would not be embarrassed by the show of affection and sympathy. She took everything at face value – even monsters, it seemed.

The creature was badly scorched, its long fur now a shrivelled mass. One great paw was extended along the tunnel, as if he had been hitting out at Mr Fredericks. The hair had burned away from round its claws to reveal the flesh below. The skin was blistered from the heat. Burned away like thin paper.

'Poor Ratty,' Flinch said quietly, before turning and hiding her face in Meg's shoulder.

Meg held her tight and let her cry. She could see that there was still a slight movement in the creature's body – a last few trembling breaths. But in a little while it would certainly be dead and there was no point in letting Flinch know how it might be suffering.

Art and Jonny had gone quiet. Meg could see them stooped over another body. If she strained, she could see the face of the man, but she did not want to. She could imagine already how it must look. Whether the creature had killed its former master before the fire consumed them both, she neither knew nor cared. The man was dead and that was an end to it.

Or almost. 'How are we going to get out of here?' Meg asked.

'Well, I was hoping we could persuade Ratty to dig us out through the fall in the tunnel,' Art said.

'Unlikely,' Jonny said quietly.

Art nodded. 'So we'll just have to use my other plan.' He was grinning in that infuriatingly smug way he had when he knew he was ahead of them.

Even Flinch had detected his note of self-satisfaction and pulled away from Meg. They all got to their feet. Meg was not going to be the one to give him an excuse to show off, she decided.

'All right,' Jonny said at last. 'What's this amazing plan, then?'

'I'd have thought it was pretty obvious. Mr Fredericks told us how to get out of here.'

'Did he?' Meg asked, despite herself.

But Art did not answer. He just smiled, and turned and walked off down the tunnel. After several moments, the others followed him.

They had managed to shore up the roof of the tunnel with planks supported by wooden pillars. The scheme relied on the bricks remaining firmly enough in place for the makeshift scaffolding to stay jammed to the roof rather than merely forcing the brickwork apart.

But digging away the fallen rubble was less straightforward. Constable Atkins and three other policemen had been working at it for the best part of an hour. Sergeant Drake was sitting exhausted, depressed and anxious on the floor of the tunnel. The whole site was illuminated by hurricane lamps that threw distorted shadows across the rubble. The working policemen became angular, broken monsters as they shovelled and heaved at the debris. But to very little effect.

They had hardly made an impression. Whenever they managed to move one section of the pile, another part of the roof fell in from behind. It might well be, Drake thought, that their efforts were serving only to make the problem worse. What was more, he had no real reason to suppose that the children and PC Wilkins were trapped in the tunnel anyway.

Probably they had never gone down there. And even if they had, then they had probably come out again. And if they had not come out again, they would probably have found another exit by now. Probably. But there always remained the possibility that Art and his friends were trapped behind, or even below, the fallen section of sewer.

'Sir?' He could tell from his tone that Constable Rogers had already called him once.

'Sorry, Rogers, I was miles away.'

Rogers shifted uncomfortably. 'I'm afraid you need to be, sir. Well, maybe not miles.' He was frowning as he watched his colleagues struggling to make an impression on the blocked tunnel.

'What do you mean? And what are you doing down here anyway?'

'That's it, sir. A message. From Mr Hanbury at the bank. You know, sir, Hanbury and Hedges, the bank where –'

'I know which bank,' Drake snapped back. 'Get to the point, please.' He was tired and he was anxious.

'He wants you to come at once, sir. He's just got to the bank to open up ready for the staff to arrive for work.' Rogers paused, as if not sure quite how to explain the problem.

'And?'

'And there's something in the vault, sir. He's

afraid to open up in case it's the robbers. He says he doesn't want to scare them off.'

'Doesn't want them to scare him off, more like.' Drake got to his feet, fatigue gone. Here was something he could do. And there was the beginnings of a thought at the back of his mind of how it might help to find Art.

'Leave that,' Drake called to the working policemen. 'I think we're wasting our time here anyway.'

They dropped their shovels and stepped back, grateful for the break.

'You haven't got time to loiter about,' Drake told them. 'We're needed at Hanbury and Hedges Bank.'

It was still early, but several employees were already sorting through papers and preparing for the day's work. They looked up, nervous and surprised, as Sergeant Drake and several policemen walked in through the main doors.

Whether they were surprised simply to see the policemen return or by the state of their dusty uniforms and muddy faces, Drake could not tell. Being a detective, he was not in uniform himself.

But he was aware that he had lost a button from his jacket, his face was plastered in dirt and his trouser legs were soaked with sewer water up to above the knees. He was also conscious of the clinging smell of the drains that was emanating from his colleagues, and could only conclude that he smelled at least as bad.

As if in confirmation of this suspicion, the clerk who approached them seemed to catch his breath and his nose wrinkled. He made an effort to control himself and managed to explain that Mr Hanbury was waiting outside the vault.

Hanbury's eyes widened and his beard twitched when he saw Drake and the others approach him.

'Investigations are continuing,' Drake told him. He offered no further explanation. 'Now, what have we got here, then?'

'Listen,' Hanbury said, and gestured for Drake to put his head close to the closed door of the vault.

Drake listened. At first he could hear nothing. But then his ears picked out what sounded like a high-pitched squeak. Some animal perhaps, trapped inside the vault. But then he realised that what he had taken for the sound of the lift behind him moving back up to the floor above was actually coming from the vault door. A banging, tapping sound. Rhythmic, but not mechanical, as there was a variation in the intervals between the sounds.

'Someone's knocking on the door,' he said in disbelief.

'There can't be anyone in there,' Hanbury said, staring at the heavy metal door. 'It's been locked. There just can't be.' He turned to Drake. 'What do we do?' he whispered.

'Well,' Drake said, 'when someone knocks on your door, it's polite to open it.'

Hanbury seemed too nervous to open the door himself, so Drake got PC Atkins to turn the large key and draw back the heavy bolts. The sound from the other side stopped as the bolts scraped across the metal.

The door swung slowly inwards on well-oiled hinges. Hanbury gave a gasp of astonishment at what was revealed inside. Atkins gave a short, sharp laugh of disbelief. Drake himself smiled and shook his head. 'Hello, Flinch,' he said.

The girl was grinning hugely. She looked a

mess – more of a mess than usual. There was no doubt that she too had spent a long time down in the sewer tunnels. Her clothes were torn and stained, her hair was matted and had bits of moss and straw and goodness knew what else lodged in it. But despite her appearance, Drake did not mind that she ran forwards and hugged him.

'Art and the others,' she said breathlessly, 'they're still in the tunnels. They couldn't get through the wood and stuff.' She led them through the vault to where the hole into the sewers had been barricaded over. She pointed to an impossibly narrow opening between two planks of wood. 'I squeezed through here,' she said proudly. 'Easy.'

'Who is it, Flinch?' came a muffled shout from the other side of the wooden wall. 'Did you get someone?'

'Is that you in there, Arthur Drake?' Sergeant Drake called.

There was a pause, then the voice answered sheepishly, 'Er, Dad?'

'I suppose this is what you call going straight home to bed.' But Drake was smiling with relief as he said it. 'All right, you lot,' he told the policemen, 'let's have this opened up and get them out of there.'

Several minutes later, Art, Meg and Jonny climbed out of the tunnels and into the bank vault. For a moment, the children looked at the policemen who had removed the wooden barricade, and the policemen looked at them, and then they all started to laugh.

The only person who did not laugh was Mr Hanbury. He watched them with open-mouthed amazement, then he shook his head and went back to the lift.

'Like I said, Dad,' Art explained, when he had recovered enough to speak. 'It's a long story.'

'Yes,' Meg agreed. 'You see, there was this dead cat.'

'Tiger,' said Flinch.

'A dead tiger?' Art's dad said.

'And Mr Fredericks wasn't really Mr Fredericks at all,' Jonny added. 'He had this monster.'

'Which robbed the bank,' Art said, as if this explained everything. 'Oh, and there's a leaking gas main down there. Jonny plugged it with a wet hanky, but we need to turn the gas off before it ignites.'

'Again,' put in Meg.

'And all the money's down there too, of course,' Jonny added.

'But Ratty's dead,' Flinch said sadly.

'I think,' Sergeant Drake said loudly over the children's overlapping explanations, 'that what we need to do is this.' He waited until they were quiet before he went on, counting off the items on his grubby fingers. 'Atkins and Rogers, you get into those tunnels and sort out this gas pipe. Jonny can tell you where it is.' He paused for Jonny to nod his agreement. 'Art and Meg and Jonny and Flinch can come home with me and have a sit-down and a cup of tea, while Art explains exactly what they've been up to and what's happening here.' Again he waited for their nods of agreement before he went on. 'Then I think we all need a good long rest. And,' he added, 'a good long bath.'

Art grinned. 'Thanks, Dad.'

Jonny was already explaining to an unenthusiastic PC Atkins how to find the tunnel where the gas pipe was broken.

Meg stood with her arms folded, watching

them and trying not to smile.

Flinch looked at each of her friends in turn, her expression a mixture of surprise and outrage. 'I don't need no bath,' she said.

Arthur knew the code to unlock the door, as of course did his grandad. It was after midnight when they let themselves quietly in and tiptoed along the sterile-smelling corridor to Grandad's room.

There was a nurse on duty in the office, but she was busy with paperwork and did not hear them sneak past. The door to Grandad's room was standing open and they slipped inside, closing it quietly behind them.

'You sure you'll be all right?' Arthur wanted to know.

'I'll get my knuckles rapped for wandering off,' Grandad told him with a wry smile. 'It's like being back at school in here, you know. But I'll tell them I had things to attend to and to mind their own business.'

'Won't they be cross?'

Grandad gave a chuckle at the thought. 'What can they do? Send me home?' His smile faded. 'No, your father will be more of a challenge, though.' He frowned thoughtfully. 'He asks altogether too many questions... A bit like you and me.'

'Family trait,' Arthur said. 'He is a policeman, after all. If it helps, I can tell him you mentioned it to me and I forgot. That you had some business, I mean, and had to go away for a couple of days.'

Grandad shook his head. 'No, no, no. It will be fine.' He took Arthur's hands in his own, and Arthur could feel that they were dry and rough with age. 'I shall tell him I went to stay with Harry Jerrickson at the antiques shop. He's an old friend.' His smile was back now. 'But then, you know that.'

'Jerrickson?' Arthur said slowly. 'But isn't that...?'

'A story for another day?' Grandad finished for him. 'Yes, well, perhaps it is. Perhaps it is.' He let go of Arthur's hands and stood up. 'Now, I think it's time you were getting home to bed. I'm quite old enough to manage on my own now, thank you.'

'I know that,' Arthur told him. 'I've seen for myself.'

The two policemen splashed through the tunnels, the light of their torches playing over the curved walls. PC Atkins led the way, with Rogers following nervously behind. They found the tunnel Jonny had described without difficulty. The walls were coated with a thin film of soot.

'You can smell the gas,' Atkins said.

As they approached, they could hear it too. A quiet hiss in the near-silence. Atkins inspected the pipe, a handkerchief clasped over his nose and mouth.

'Actually, I don't think it's too bad,' he told Rogers when he jumped down from the ledge. 'But we need them to shut off the supply and mend the pipe pretty sharpish.'

'Let's get back, then.'

'In a minute,' Atkins said. 'I want to have a quick look at this monster. It's only in the next tunnel.'

'Monster,' Rogers muttered. 'Kids' imagination, more like.'

They could see the body – a dark shape lying on the floor of the tunnel. It was the body of a middle-aged man, his features blackened by the fire and his neck broken. Atkins stooped down by the body to check that it was dead.

'Told you,' Rogers said. 'Imagination. Just this bloke, not a monster to be found.'

'Maybe,' Atkins replied. He reached out and closed the dead man's eyes. 'But something happened down here.' Even as he spoke there was a faint echoing sound from back down the tunnel. Something that sounded like a cross between a shriek and a roar... Or a wild animal calling for its mate.

The
Invisible
Detective

The Paranormal Puppet Show
The first incredible adventure for The Invisible Detective

London, 1936: The Invisible Detective can solve any mystery, great or small – but no one's ever seen his face. Truth is, the detective is the creation of four extraordinary kids who combat crime in his name…

PUPPETS THAT KILL

When a spooky exhibition comes to town, Art and the gang must deal with disappearing people, faceless bodies and some very deadly puppets… Can the Invisible Detective thwart a plot to bring the whole country to its knees?

Meanwhile, in the present day, a fourteen-year-old boy discovers the Invisible Detective's old casebook. It was written in the 1930s – but it's in his handwriting…

The
Invisible
Detective

Ghost Soldiers
The third amazing investigation for The Invisible Detective

London, 1936: The Invisible Detective can solve any mystery, great or small – but no one's ever seen his face. Truth is, the detective is the creation of four extraordinary kids who combat crime in his name...

A GHOSTLY PRESENCE

Investigating a strange death and a haunted house, Art and his friends learn there are monsters on the streets of London, dressed as soldiers and trained to kill. Can even the Invisible Detective stop the Ghost Soldiers?

And why is Arthur Drake, a boy from the London of today, reliving this horror from the past – almost as if he'd been there...?

The
Invisible
Detective

Killing Time

The fourth exciting adventure for The Invisible Detective

London, 1937: The Invisible Detective can solve any mystery, great or small – but no one's ever seen his face. Truth is, the detective is the creation of four extraordinary kids who combat crime in his name…

TIME'S RUNNING OUT

A pocket watch that seems to rewind time itself leads the gang to investigate a strange clock shop. Why are the shop's customers so strange? How are events linked to a shipwreck in Cornwall? Only the Invisible Detective can find out…

But while on holiday in the Cornwall of today, Arthur Drake's past life is catching up with him. The ghosts of sailors shipwrecked over a century ago are coming to call… but what do they want?